PRAISE FOR

SVEN CARTER

& THE TRASHMOUTH EFFECT

"Sven and his friends are the perfect motley crew of outcasts determined to save the world. . . . Over the top and full of laughs."

—SCHOOL LIBRARY JOURNAL

"A page-turner that's entertaining right down to the Acknowledgments section. Hand this fast-paced romp to an adventurer in the making."

—BULLETIN OF THE CENTER FOR CHILDREN'S BOOKS

SVEN CARTER
& THE ANDROID ARMY

CHECK OUT SVEN'S FIRST ADVENTURE:

SVEN CARTER &

THE TRASHMOUTH EFFECT

Sven Carter & the Android Army

ROB VLOCK

ALADDIN MAX
NEW YORK LONDON TORONTO SYDNEY NEW DELHI

ALADDIN MAX
Simon & Schuster Children's Publishing Division
1230 Avenue of the Americas, New York, New York 10020
First Aladdin MAX edition October 2018

Also available in an Aladdin hardcover edition.

Cover designed by Karin Paprocki
Interior designed by Mike Rosamilia
The text of this book was set in Adobe Caslon Pro.
Manufactured in the United States of America 0918 OFF
2 4 6 8 10 9 7 5 3 1
Library of Congress Cataloging-in-Publication Data
Names: Vlock, Rob, author.
Title: Sven Carter & the android army / by Rob Vlock.
Other titles: Sven Carter and the android army
Description: First Aladdin MAX edition. | New York : Aladdin MAX, 2018. |
Summary: When cyborg Sven Carter learns that he is not the only Tick, he speeds across the country gathering the others to convince them to join him in saving the world.
Identifiers: LCCN 2018017353 (print) | LCCN 2018023129 (eBook) |
ISBN 9781481490184 (eBook) | ISBN 9781481490177 (hc) | ISBN 9781481490160 (pbk)
Subjects: | CYAC: Cyborgs—Fiction. | Androids—Fiction. | Heroes—Fiction. |
Adventure and adventurers—Fiction. | Science fiction. | Humorous stories. |
BISAC: JUVENILE FICTION / Science Fiction. | JUVENILE FICTION /
Action & Adventure / General. | JUVENILE FICTION / Humorous Stories.
Classification: LCC PZ7.1.V63 (eBook) | LCC PZ7.1.V63 Sve 2018 (print) |
DDC [Fic]—dc23
LC record available at https://lccn.loc.gov/2018017353

For Mom and Dad. Thanks for making me.

And for making me who I am.

CONTENTS

CHAPTER 1.0:
\ < value= [Face, Meet Anvil] \ >

WHO KNEW THAT THE TOUGHEST PERSON I'd ever met would melt into a pile of goo three words into a song?

Actually, that's not exactly true. She hadn't *entirely* melted into a pile of goo. Because a pile of goo didn't have a fist that felt like a five-hundred-pound anvil slamming into your face.

I reached this insight—about the anvil, not the goo—the moment Alicia Toth's right fist plowed into my face and felled me as efficiently as Godzilla kicking over a miniature Eiffel Tower made of toothpicks.

I should probably explain. Let me rewind a bit.

Junkman Sam's ancient motor home creaked and groaned as it lurched along I-90. Niagara Falls was two hours behind us. Schenectady was two hours ahead.

I stared out the window, even though there was nothing to look at. It wasn't light yet, so the only view I had was the reflection of my own face in the glass. When the occasional car would blow by our slow-moving rust bucket, its headlights washed me out of existence for a moment or two until my face reappeared in the darkened window.

"You're sure he said that, Sven?" Alicia asked for the fifth time. "Those were his exact words?"

For the fifth time, I gave her the same answer. "Yes. I'm sure. He asked if I ever wondered why I was called Seven. Then he laughed and said, 'A little something for you to ponder when you think of me.' Only with more stuttering and gurgling because his head was hanging from a gigantic electromagnet."

"You're *sure*?" Alicia repeated.

I sighed and went back to looking out the window.

Dr. Shallix, the cybernetic mastermind behind *srok rasplaty*—the day of reckoning—a plot to extinguish every human life on Earth, had been dead for hours. Yet he was still making my life miserable. It wasn't easy coming to terms with the fact that I'd been Shallix's superweapon—a pawn in his evil plan.

"Maybe he didn't mean there are other Ticks out there waiting to kill everyone on the planet," Will suggested hopefully. "Maybe he just meant they screwed up the first six Ticks they tried to build. You know, like it took them seven tries to get it right." He ran an oversize hand through his tousled red hair in a way that suggested he didn't believe it himself.

Alicia rounded on him. "And are you willing to bet six billion lives on that?" she snapped.

Before Will could answer, Junkman Sam cleared his throat and called back to us from the driver's seat. "I think it's reasonable to assume that since Sven was designated Seven Omicron, there are other Synthetics like him in the Omicron line."

The color drained out of Will's face. "Wait! You're

saying there are six more Ticks like Sven out there waiting to exterminate all humans?"

Junkman Sam shrugged. "No, I'm not saying that."

A long, relieved sigh escaped Will's lips.

Sam continued. "Could be six more. Could be six hundred. Who knows?"

Will's sigh turned into a kind of strangled moan. He started flipping an old ashtray open and closed.

That was kind of Will's thing. He had OCD. Obsessive-compulsive disorder. So when he was scared or stressed or upset, he'd do these little rituals. You know, like turning light switches on and off. Or opening and closing doors. Stuff like that.

Of course, compared to *my* thing, Will's thing was nothing. I ate stuff. Gross stuff. Like, for example, a wad of old gum stuck in the ashtray Will was messing with.

"You think they're all programmed to do the same thing as Sven?" Alicia asked, watching me nearly break my teeth on the decades-old gum. "Incubate superviruses that'll wipe out humanity?"

Sam scratched his stubbly chin. "Maybe. They may

have mass-produced that model and designed each one to function as a disease vector."

Alicia bit her lip nervously. "If there are that many of those things running around, we're in big trouble."

Things. That's what I was. A thing that was made, not born. A weapon. A Synthetic humanlike object. Thinking about it made my stomach turn.

I walked to the front of the motor home and turned on the radio. I didn't care what was on. Anything was better than hearing my friends talk about me like I was a *thing*.

Okay, I take that back. Because Dixon Watts was singing. As usual, it sounded just like a cat that had gotten its tail caught in the door.

Girl, you're as fine as some really smooth sandpaper.
I want to kiss your face more than a lightsaber.

I reached out to turn to another station.

Junkman Sam's right hand flew off the steering wheel and slapped my arm away from the radio. "Hey, I love this song."

I stared at him like he had just told me his father was an onion bagel. "You're joking, right?" I asked, somehow knowing he wasn't joking. "I mean, you *have* to understand just how much this song sucks."

"Dude, shut up!" Will barked. "This tune is awesome!"

Girl, I love you like a dog loves its kibble.

Why can't you love me back just a libble?

"Come on!" I protested. "Listen to it! 'Libble' isn't even a word! He's terrible!"

Alicia scowled at me. "Take that back! Dix is amazing!"

"Yeah, you must be the only person on Earth who doesn't love him!" Will added.

"A few weeks ago you didn't even know who he was!" I countered.

It was true. A month ago, nobody on the planet had heard of Dixon Watts. Then he burst onto the scene like a mushy jack-o'-lantern in December, the biggest teen-pop mega-superstar in the history of music. His song

"Girl, You Are My Shredded Wheat" was at the top spot on every chart in the world. And spots two through twelve on those charts were filled with the other songs from his first album. You couldn't go anywhere without hearing one of those ear-manglers.

"How can you listen to this?" I pressed. "He sounds like a blender full of quarters! No, you know what he sounds like? A garbage disposal full of forks. He's the worst singer—"

I didn't get to finish the sentence. Because that was the moment Alicia's anvil of a fist smashed into my face.

The only good thing about being knocked out by Alicia Toth was that I was unconscious for the rest of Dixon Watts's song. When I opened my eyes a few minutes later, I was relieved to hear the DJ's voice oozing in that slick, plasticky tone pop station radio announcers all like to use.

"That was Dix Watts's mega-superhit 'Girl, You Are My Shredded Wheat.' But don't you dare turn off your radio! Because we've just gotten a brand-new surprise release from Dix! Here is 'Babe, You Are My Scrambled Eggs'!"

One of the worst things I'd ever heard came warbling out of the RV's speakers.

Babe, you are my scrambled eggs!
I love you and your bacon legs!

"Haven't I suffered enough?" I blurted through a fat lip, instantly wishing I could bite back the words as I thought about Alicia's fist and its run-in with my face. What was up with her, anyway? I mean sure, Alicia punching people wasn't all that unusual. But because of a song? That was a bit much, even for her.

So just relax and don't put up a fight.
'Cause you know it's gonna be all right.

But Alicia just sat perfectly still with a weird, vacant look on her face. So did Will and Sam. It was like they were in a trance.

I cleared my throat. "Uh, guys?" I said tentatively.

They ignored me.

"Guys!" I shouted. "Are you okay?"

Will turned and fixed a pair of glazed eyes on me. "Okay? Yeah. Better than okay. Amaaaaazing."

He said the words flatly, mechanically, drawing out the final *A* like it was an ice-cream cone he was savoring.

"Will? What's going on? A few minutes ago you were about to have a freak-out over the other Ticks out there. Now you're amazing?"

"Ticks?" Alicia intoned emotionlessly. "You know, I've been thinking they're not all that bad. I don't know why we were all worried about them."

Not all that bad? Alicia's parents died at the hands of Ticks back when she lived at the Settlement in the Chernobyl exclusion zone. And you saw how she got when I insulted a song she liked. What was going on here?

Yeah, don't hate, don't fight, don't push,

don't shove.

Just have a stack of pancake love.

The song! It was doing something to my friends!

I grabbed Will by the shoulders and shook him. "Will! Come on! Wake up!"

But he just stared straight ahead with a half smile on his face.

"Alicia!" I cried. "Are you with me?"

I slapped her. Normally, something like that probably would have resulted in one or more of my bones being broken. But all Alicia did was sing along with the chorus:

Babe, you are my scrambled eggs!
I love you and your bacon legs!

Ohh-kay.

Time for plan B.

I reached for the volume knob.

Without warning, Junkman Sam sprang from his seat and clamped me into a headlock, his sweat-stained armpit pressing against my ear as he wrestled me away from the radio.

One thought managed to break through the din: *Nobody's driving the motor home!*

A grinding sound echoed through the vehicle as we plowed through a guardrail.

All of a sudden, the world was upside down. Instead of the blacktop illuminated by the headlights, all I could see through the windshield were clumps of grass and shrubs. Freed from Sam's grip as the vehicle jolted and careened, I latched my arm around the back of the passenger seat to try to keep from being smashed to a pulp. The motor home convulsed once . . . twice . . . three times, as it hit little dips on the way down the slope . . . and slammed directly into a tree.

CHAPTER 2.0:

\ < value= [RV, Meet Tree] \ >

WILL AND I WENT TO CAMP ONE SUMMER where they had this huge rock-climbing wall. It must have been fifty feet tall.

Our counselor, a tall, skinny, pimple-faced teenager named Ernie, prided himself on his reassuring way with the campers.

"Don't worry about falling off," he'd told us with a laugh. "It's not the fall that'll kill you. It's the sudden stop at the end."

So I guess it was lucky for those of us in Junkman Sam's RV that there was no sudden stop at the end of our brief, yet utterly terrifying, off-road excursion.

The tree we plowed into turned out to be half-rotted, barely slowing the vehicle at all. Its trunk snapped off about two feet from the ground, no match for the twelve thousand pounds of rusty metal slamming into it.

The vehicle juddered to a stop. Its engine spluttered and coughed a few times and then went silent.

Will, who had been thrown to the floor, stood up and blinked. "Wha-what happened?"

"And why did we stop?" Alicia added, looking out the window. "Where are we?"

"What the heck?" I cried. "What's wrong with you people?"

Alicia squinted at me. "Wrong with us? What are you talking about?"

I glared at her. "Seriously? You don't remember?"

"Remember what?" Junkman Sam scratched his frizzled mop of hair. "Last I knew we were just west of Syracuse, on our way to Shallix's office to find out how many other Ticks . . . uh, I mean *people* like you might be out there."

"So you don't remember the Dixon Watts song?" I asked incredulously.

"Well, I remember punching you because you were saying some *very* unfair things about one of Dixon's songs, if that's what you mean," Alicia replied. Then she paused. "Which I guess was probably a little over-the-top. Sorry. But, you know . . . Dixon."

"No, not that one. I mean the song that was playing when we crashed. The one about the scrambled eggs."

All three of them stared at me blankly.

"Scrambled eggs?" Will scrunched his eyebrows together. "Haven't heard that one. But it sounds great."

"It isn't!" I snapped. "You guys were . . . *weird* when it was on. Like you were in a trance or something. I tried to turn the radio off and Sam jumped on me. That's why we crashed."

"I don't remember that." Sam furrowed his brow. "But it doesn't sound like something I would do."

"You did," I assured him. "And Alicia, you said Ticks weren't that bad."

Her face darkened. "No way I'd say that."

"Listen to me. It was the song. It had some kind of hold over you." I turned to Will and Sam. "Over all of you."

Alicia opened her mouth, then closed it again.

"Maybe we shouldn't listen to the radio anymore," Will suggested quietly, going back to nervously flipping the ashtray open and closed.

Junkman Sam turned the key in the ignition.

Nothing happened.

"Listening to the radio won't be an option unless we can get the motor home running." He grabbed a flashlight from the glove compartment, squeezed past me, and placed his hand on the RV's side door. He paused. "Of course, the bigger problem is that if we can't get on the road soon, we'll never get to Shallix's office before sunup. And I don't particularly fancy the idea of breaking and entering in the light of day."

He slipped out into the night.

By the time we followed him out, Junkman Sam had already squirmed halfway under the vehicle. His generous belly and stumpy legs protruded from beneath the front bumper.

"Ja nadejus' tebe deti v sup polujut!" he snarled.

I didn't need to understand a word of Russian to know he wasn't happy. I looked to Alicia for a translation.

"An old Russian saying," she informed me. "It's more or less 'I hope your children poop in your soup.'"

Sam wriggled out from under the RV. "Half of our electrical system was torn out by that stump."

"Can you fix it?" I asked.

He tugged on his earlobe thoughtfully. "Let's hope so."

Alicia looked at the lights of a passing car. "Can't we just hitchhike to Schenectady or something? Or call a cab?"

Sam shook his head. "My equipment is in the motor home. I think we're going to need it if we want to hack into Shallix's records and learn the full extent of his plot."

While he worked on the vehicle, Alicia turned to me. "Tell me more about that song you mentioned. What did it sound like?"

"It sounded the same as every other Dixon Watts song. You know, like a hippo with diarrhea, or maybe . . ."

Alicia's glare stopped the words in my throat.

"Do I need to punch you again?"

I spoke softly in an effort not to enrage her. "I'm not trying to make you mad. But I genuinely think Dixon Watts might be tone-deaf."

I took a step back as Alicia's face reddened.

"Well," she snapped. "Maybe you just don't get his music—you ever think of that? Maybe I hear something in his songs that you don't!"

As soon as she said it, an idea hit me. "Wait! Maybe you're right!"

She nodded smugly. "Of course I'm right! Dix's songs are awesome."

"No, no. Not that. But maybe you're right about hearing something in it that I can't. Think about it. What's the biggest difference between you two and me?"

"We're human," Alicia answered.

"And I'm Synthetic," I added.

Will drummed his fingers on the side of the RV. "Wait, are you saying you hear music differently than we do because you're a Tick?"

"Maybe he just has terrible taste in music," Alicia suggested.

I rolled my eyes. "There's nothing wrong with my taste in music. But there's nothing remotely musical about Dixon Watts! I'd rather listen to nails on a chalkboard."

"Phhffft!" Alicia huffed. "I bet you're probably not programmed to appreciate how great Dix is."

"What?"

"She has a point," Will chimed in. "It's probably just . . . you know, his greatness overloads your music enjoyment circuits or something."

Okay, *that* was annoying!

"You know what?" I fumed, my fingernails digging into the palms of my tightly clenched fists. "Forget it! Let's not talk about it anymore!"

I marched to the door of the motor home, wrenched it open, and slumped onto the cracked vinyl of the passenger seat. Hot anger welled inside my throat.

There it was again. My friends treating me like I was inhuman just because I happened not to be human.

I nearly died to save them! What did it matter that I had a CPU instead of a brain? I still had feelings!

Add to that the fact that a half-baked replica of me with a face where his butt should be was taking my place at home with my parents while I was out here listening to Alicia and Will reminding me of how utterly alone I was. . . .

My anger morphed into soul-crushing despair. I was alone. And nobody could ever understand what it was like to be me.

Then, out of the furthest, darkest corner of my mind came a voice. Tiny. Barely audible at all. But still powerful enough to pierce the blackness.

Kill them all.

CHAPTER 3.0:

\ < value= [Our Plan Goes Up in Smoke] \ >

THE MOTOR HOME'S DOOR CREAKED OPEN.

"You okay, Sven?" Will asked apologetically.

An explosion of razor-sharp hate detonated in my skull.

Them!

My fingers closed on the arms of my chair until the vinyl skin crackled. A millisecond later, the voice was gone. Completely.

I loosened my grip on the chair and smiled feebly at my friends. "Uh . . . I'm fine." But the words sounded more like a question than an answer. "How's Sam doing?" I added, trying to occupy my mind with questions other than *What the heck just happened?*

Alicia shrugged. "Well, he's no longer talking about poop in the soup, so that's a positive sign. Although I might have just heard him say someone had onions growing out of their belly button, which . . . I don't know how to interpret, actually."

As if he were summoned by the mention of his name, Junkman Sam hoisted himself up into the RV with a wheezy grunt.

"Did you fix it?" Will asked.

"Only one way to find out." Sam muttered something under his breath and inserted the key into the ignition.

"Wait!" I cried, and made sure the radio was off. "Okay, I think we're good."

Sam crossed his fingers and gave the key a twist.

A horrifying moaning, whining sound filled the air. It turned out it was only the motor home's engine rumbling to life.

Sam scowled at a couple of gauges on the dashboard and wiped his brow. "Well, I guess it worked."

We slowly ground our way back up the embankment toward the mangled gap in the guardrail. Finally, when we were once again on the road, I settled onto the lumpy couch, closed my eyes, and pretended to be asleep.

It wasn't long before I wasn't pretending.

I was jolted awake by the flush of the morning sun slanting through the RV's windows.

"What time is it?" I wondered aloud, too tired to open my eyes.

"Three thirty," Alicia's voice answered.

"And where are we?"

"Schenectady."

"Wait. Hold on." Sleepy cobwebs disintegrated just enough to let the gears of logic shudder into motion. "If . . . if it's three thirty in the morning, why . . . why is the sun out?"

"It's not."

My eyelids shot open and I rubbed away a couple of crusty eye boogers, which I promptly licked off my fingers. *Gross.*

I looked outside and realized it wasn't sunshine I had felt on my face. It was the angry glow of flames.

What was left of Dr. Shallix's office was on fire.

I looked at Alicia. “Did you do this?” Given Alicia’s tendency to blow things up or burn things down on a fairly regular basis, it seemed like a fair question.

“It was like that when we got here.”

I watched the side wall of the building collapse, sending up a blizzard of orange embers. “What happened?”

Junkman Sam opened the door. “Let’s find out.”

We stepped out onto the sidewalk and made our way toward the inferno, careful to avoid stumbling over the firehoses that snaked across Union Street.

“Stay back!” a firefighter commanded. She wore the white helmet of a fire chief.

“What happened here?” Sam asked.

“Gas leak,” the woman told us. “The whole building exploded. That’s why you have to get out of the area *now*! For all we know, this entire block could still go up!”

From her tone, I knew there was no arguing with her. Besides, there was no way we’d be able to get anything useful out of Dr. Shallix’s office now.

We filed back toward the motor home, and I leaned, dejected, against its dented side.

Alicia put words to the thought that must have been going through all of our minds. "No way that was a gas leak. Shallix must have planned this in case he didn't come back from Niagara Falls. He didn't want to leave any evidence behind."

"What do we do now?" Will's eyes were wide. "That was our only lead!"

Sam shook his head slowly. "What can we do? We have no idea what the full extent of Shallix's plot was. We don't know who's involved." He glanced at me. "We don't even know who's human and who's a Tick."

The four of us stood in silence, the weight of despair stilling our tongues.

Until a firefighter paused near our position to adjust his helmet. "Girl, you're as fine as some really smooth sandpaper. I want to kiss your face more than a light-saber," he sang in a deep baritone voice.

And a second later, my friends joined in.

"Girl, I love you like a dog loves its kibble.

Why can't you love me back just a libble?"

"It's . . . it's Dixon Watts!" I blurted.

"Yeah, he's awesome." The firefighter nodded at me, gave his helmet strap one more tug, and continued on his way.

"No, I mean that's what we need to do. We have to see Dixon Watts!"

Alicia rolled her eyes. "Good luck with that. Every show for the next year sold out two minutes after tickets went on sale."

"Besides," Will added, "I thought you hated him."

"I do," I agreed. "And I'm not talking about seeing him perform. I just . . . I think he's involved somehow with Dr. Shallix's plot."

"Please!" Alicia snapped. "Just because you have no taste in music doesn't mean Dixon is working with the Ticks."

I turned to her. "You didn't see how you were acting when that song of his was on! He's involved somehow. I know it!"

"I think you're grasping at straws."

"True. But do you have a better idea?"

"I can think of worse things than meeting Dixon

Watts," Junkman Sam said, half to himself. "He's such a dreamboat. Maybe he'll sign my underwear."

Will, Alicia, and I trained our collective gaze on Sam.

His face flushed crimson. "Did I say that aloud? Uh . . . uh, what I meant was, uh . . . he's a very talented musician and Sven might be onto something."

Alicia sighed. "All right. There's no reason to stick around here, anyway."

As if to emphasize her point, the sole remaining wall of the burning building crumbled to the ground.

CHAPTER 4.0:
\ < value= [Roadkill] \ >

"MADISON SQUARE GARDEN," ALICIA announced, looking up from her phone. "He's playing two weeks of sold-out shows there, starting tonight."

Junkman Sam started up the RV. "That's good luck. New York City is just a few hours from here. We'll be there in time for breakfast."

Will's stomach rumbled loudly at the mention of breakfast. "Yeah, but we're going to need more than luck if we want to actually meet Dixon Watts in person. I bet he has the toughest bodyguards in the music business."

"That's a problem," Sam agreed. "But I'm sure once we explain why we want to see him, they'll let us through."

Will snorted. "You mean once we explain how there's a secret race of androids that's planning to wipe out every person on Earth and we think Dixon might be somehow involved because Sven doesn't like his music?"

Sam scratched his nose. "I suppose it couldn't hurt to have a plan B."

Right around Poughkeepsie, I noticed the black shadow.

I had taken to staring out the window while trying to come up with a plan B. I had just killed the idea of dressing up in bear costumes and telling the bodyguards we were there to deliver a singing telegram when I spotted a blur of motion from the corner of my eye.

I strained against the darkness to try to make out what I had seen, but there was nothing there. Just an endless rush of shadowy green trees faintly illuminated by the distant, cold light of the stars.

Then I saw it again: a dark streak keeping pace with the RV about twenty feet away.

I couldn't fix it in my vision. It almost felt like the idea of something rather than the thing itself. Every time

I tried to focus on it, it blended into the shadows and disappeared. But the hairs on the back of my neck stood up. Like they could sense we were being watched.

"Guys!" I called. "Can you take a look outside? I think there's something—"

The motor home's tires screeched on the asphalt, then . . . *THUMP!* The RV bucked like an angry bull.

"A deer! It . . . it just ran out in front of us!" Sam wailed, his voice soaked with anguish. "We have to see if it's okay."

I nodded, even though I already knew that deer wasn't okay. No way a deer could be okay after getting flattened by the old hunk we were riding in.

The vehicle slowed to a stop on the shoulder of the road. Sam shifted into park and unbuckled himself from the driver's seat. "Maybe we can help it. Take it to a vet if it's . . ." His voice shook with emotion.

"Sam . . . ," Alicia began. She sighed. "Yeah, maybe we can do something."

She got up from the couch. But not before sliding her knife out of her backpack.

The sight of the blade glinting in the RV's overhead lights sent a jolt of ice down my spine. "What's that for?"

Alicia paused at the door and swallowed hard. "In case it's . . . suffering."

I stared at her. "You mean you'll put it out of its misery? Can you . . . would you really be able to do that?"

She grimaced. "I don't know."

I joined her at the door and gave her shoulder a squeeze. I couldn't stand the thought of what she was suggesting. But I also couldn't let her go through that alone.

We stepped out into the cool night air.

"Over here!" Junkman Sam called.

Alicia let out a long breath and took a step toward Sam and the deer. I followed right behind.

The deer's long, delicate limbs were in a tangle of improbable angles. Its chest was still, its once-impressive antlers nothing more than jagged six-inch nubs.

Sam lifted his gaze. Even in the glow of his flashlight, we could read the distress on his face. "I couldn't stop. It came out of nowhere. I—I barely had time to brake at all."

He turned suddenly and trundled down the grassy verge at the side of the road, where he barfed up the contents of his stomach.

Alicia went after him.

I tore my gaze away from the animal and looked up at the stars. A streak of black blotted them out. Something passed so close to my face I could feel the wind as it rushed by.

What was that?

Before I could give it another thought, a sound at my feet drew my attention back to the road. The deer was moving. Its legs twisted and turned, disentangling themselves from one another, bones crackling as they straightened. Its hooves scraped against the pavement, carving gouges into the blacktop.

The animal scrambled to its feet and stood before me, its face still frozen in a grimace.

Until I realized it wasn't a grimace.

It was a grin.

CHAPTER 5.0:

\ < value= [Stuck in the Middle] \ >

"TARGET ACQUIRED: SEVEN OMICRON." The voice rattled out of the deer. "Commencing termination."

"Alicia!" I screamed. "I need you! Now!"

"Geez, Sven," she called back to me. "Keep your pants on. Sam's having a tough time here."

"*I'm* having a tough time!" I countered, backing away from the deer. It lowered its head and lunged at me, its broken antlers pointed at my chest.

I twisted hard to the left and narrowly avoided being skewered. Still, the animal's shoulder clipped my side and sent me whirling to the ground.

"Help!" The deer skidded to a stop and turned to take a second run at me. "Tick! It's a Tick!"

The animal shot forward. Sparks erupted where its hooves made contact with the pavement.

A millisecond before the deer trampled me into mush, I rolled toward the side of the road. But not quite fast enough. One of its hooves came down hard on my right thumb. My entire arm throbbed in pain. I clutched my bloody hand to my chest. Well, most of my hand, anyway. My thumb lay twitching all by itself on the pavement.

"Sven!" Alicia cried as she made it to the road about twenty feet away from me. Her knife was in her hand and she assumed a fighting stance.

"Secondary target acquired," the deer croaked, swiveling its head toward her. "Engaging."

The Tick streaked toward Alicia. But she was already on the move. With an almost balletic spin, she buried her blade deep in the animal's flank. The razor-sharp steel opened the creature's hide like a zipper.

It emitted an enraged squawk, but the injury closed

itself up, fading to a thread of scar tissue, then disappearing altogether. Thanks to the emergency repair system in every Tick, injuries like the one Alicia had just inflicted would barely slow the creature down at all.

I should know. I had experienced the same thing when my arm was torn off while I was trying to jump over a wedding cake on my bike. (Don't ask.) And when I had been stabbed by a trio of roast chicken assassins a couple of nights earlier—which, odd as it sounds, is precisely the type of thing that tends to happen when you have an army of cybernetic killers trying to take you out.

I scrambled up and darted to the side of the road. But then I remembered my thumb. I'd probably need that.

I scooped it up just as the deer began charging toward me. I pivoted back toward the grassy verge where Alicia waved me on frantically. But the sole of my right sneaker slipped on a piece of broken antler that lay on the pavement, and I crashed to the ground.

I gasped and coughed, struggling to catch my breath. And all I could do was watch the deer speed toward me.

It lowered its head, and I swear its lips pulled back

into a full-on smile. Its teeth glinted in the dim starlight.

Only, I realized a moment later, it wasn't starlight reflecting off the beast's teeth. It was headlights.

I looked away from the deer to find a vehicle barreling straight toward me from the opposite direction. I squinted into the headlights, but in the glare all I could make out was a large, dark, trucklike shape.

I waved my arms in a lame effort to get it to stop. But if anything, the driver only sped up.

So there I was.

On one side, a killer Synthetic deer.

On the other, several tons of speeding steel.

I caught my breath just in time to scream. But my voice was drowned out by the roar of the vehicle's engine as it closed the few remaining feet between us.

CHAPTER 6.0:

\ < value= [A Walk in the Park] \ >

THUMP!

A squeal of tires on pavement. A hulk of rusty metal passed over me, no more than two inches from the tip of my nose. It smelled like gasoline and hot steel.

When the vehicle skidded to a stop, I rolled out from under it, lifted myself unsteadily into a sitting position, and looked at the object that had nearly flattened me. It was Sam's RV.

"Sven!" Will cried as he scrambled out of the motor home. "Are you okay? I thought I might've hit you!"

I wanted to tell him that I was fine. But as I opened my mouth, a pair of words rang out in my head. *Kill him.* They were accompanied by a searing wave of fury.

"WHAT THE HECK WERE YOU DOING?!?" I bellowed. "YOU ALMOST KILLED ME!"

I stood up and shoved Will hard.

He fell to the ground.

I cocked my leg to kick at his ribs when the anger drained out of me as quickly as it had come. I stood there like a fool, perched on one leg, staring down at my best friend, who was trembling on the pavement.

"S-sorry," I stuttered, returning my foot to the ground. "I'm okay, Will. I . . . I don't know why I just did that."

I offered him my hand. He flinched.

Oh, right. My thumb. I pressed the severed digit back into place and held it there while the nanomachines that made up my blood did their work. Flesh and bone knitted together until all that was left of the injury was a red scar.

Will got unsteadily to his feet. "I—I—I saw that deer attacking you. I was trying to drive over so you could get in. I wasn't trying to hit you! I just . . . I guess I forgot which pedal was the gas and which was the brake."

"The deer!" I looked around frantically. "Where is it?"

"It's okay," Alicia called to us from the front of the RV.

She was standing beside the vehicle's passenger door, glaring at the pavement. There, under the front wheel of the motor home, lay the deer. It was pinned in place beneath the tire, squirming and struggling to get free.

"Target Reacquired: Seven Omicron." Its voice was barely audible.

Will took a step back. "Kill it! It's still alive!"

"That's what I voted for," Alicia said icily. "But Sam said he had a better idea."

Something about her tone made me think that whatever idea Sam had, I wasn't going to like it.

Junkman Sam rounded the corner of the RV and stood next to Alicia. He had a deeply apologetic look on his face.

And he was clutching a handful of electrical cables.

"I don't want to do this," I said for the twenty-third time. I knew I was going to do it, though, no matter how much the thought made my guts twist.

My head was a foot away from the deer's. The creature was still talking, its voice so low that I was the only one who could hear it.

"Seven Omicron," it repeated over and over. "Seven Omicron."

I wished it would stop. Hearing it chant my name—my Synthetic designation—was far more uncomfortable than the press of the rough pavement against my cheek as I lay on my stomach by the side of the road.

"Okay, I think we're ready." Sam had gathered what he needed. The cables, a laptop, forceps, some small magnets . . . and a scalpel. The glint of its blade in the starlight reawakened a searing sensation along the back of my neck—the precise spot Sam had cut open hours earlier, when he'd hooked that very same cable into the interface of my neural network.

"Don't worry," Will assured me in a totally unreassuring way. "I'm sure it won't hurt much."

I rolled my eyes, although the deer was probably the only one who could see it. What scared me even more than the thought of Junkman Sam cutting into my flesh for the second time in less than twenty-four hours was his harebrained plan.

"Sam, are you sure this is going to work?"

"Absolutely," he replied with no conviction whatsoever. "It worked last time, didn't it?"

"Last time you were letting me access my *own* brain, not a deer's," I reminded him. "And that almost erased my mind."

He scratched his head. "True. But I'm betting this thing doesn't have the same kind of security systems you have. You were designed to be the Ticks' ultimate instrument of human destruction. This is just a deer. It'll probably be a . . . what's the expression in English . . . ? A stroll in the nature preserve."

"A walk in the *park*," I corrected.

"Anyway, what else can we do?" Alicia argued. "Shallix's office is a hole in the ground. This is the best chance we have of finding out what the Ticks are up to."

"We could just check out Dixon Watts, like I've been saying all along."

She sat on the pavement next to me and gently put her hand on my back. "Sven, we know this deer is a Tick, right?"

I nodded and winced as my cheek scraped against the pavement.

"And I know you *think* Dix is a Tick," she continued. "But what if he's not? Or if he is, what if we can't get in to see him?" She rested her hand on my shoulder. "If there are others like you out there and we don't try everything we can to stop them . . ."

She didn't need to finish the thought. There were still Ticks out there. This deer was proof of that. And that meant the human race was still at risk of being wiped out.

"Fine." I sighed. "Let's get this over with."

"Okay," Sam responded. "Now just hold still and . . ."

Every nerve ending along the back of my neck screamed as Sam's scalpel sliced through my flesh.

CONNECTION REQUEST: </mpw

45.11.200.306.35657.44590.2 // <irq_

stat 0x220000000443 { CMWS }

08:22:60:00:tw72:02/11 // ACCESS GRANTED //

</rep [[4890553564.764_entm]] // ***DL\

C:734545689322222000-111139456832-1495555555555555555

CHAPTER 7.0:

\ < value= [Actually, a Walk in the Woods] \ >

I FOUND MYSELF LYING ON A THICK BED of pine needles staring up at sunlight slicing through a canopy of leaves. A breeze whispered through the trees. Somewhere, a bird sang a melancholy song.

I got to my feet and surveyed my surroundings. I was in a vast, dense forest that extended as far as I could see. The RV was gone. The New York State Thruway was gone. My friends were gone. Which only made sense, because I was inside the deer's brain. But I wasn't sure what I was supposed to do.

I took a step forward, snapping a dry twig under my foot. It sounded much louder than it should have. Like a gunshot. The sound set me on edge, and my body tensed instinctively, ready to break into a run.

I scanned the area for danger and noticed that I had practically a three-hundred-sixty-degree field of vision. As if I had eyes on the back of my head. Or at least on the sides of my head.

Like a deer.

Of course. I was experiencing the world the way a deer would. With a deer's hearing. A deer's vision.

And a deer's sense of smell, I discovered as the clean, sweet scent of a mountain spring wafted through the air. Suddenly, my mouth felt as if it had been filled with warm sand. I needed to find something to drink. I needed to get to that water.

Almost before I realized it, I was walking, the crisp leaves under my feet crackling in my ears. I followed the smell of the spring.

A voice in the distance called to me. *Sven! Stay in control! If you lose it now, you're dead!* But it felt miles away.

I heard the spring before I saw it. Gurgling and bubbling somewhere just ahead of me. The closer I got, the thirstier I felt. Soon, I was running, dodging tree trunks and traversing tangled roots as easily as I could have navigated the corridors of Chester A. Arthur Middle School back home in Schenectady.

As I crested a hill, a crystalline pond fed by a stream appeared in front of me, glittering in the sunshine. I dashed to the edge and stooped to take a drink. But before my lips could touch the liquid, I froze.

Something was staring up at me from just beneath the water's surface.

No. Not something. Some*one*. A man.

He looked like he was in his early twenties, with large, expressive brown eyes, heavy eyebrows, and a head covered with dark, loose curls that coiled around his ears. The man peered straight up at me from the pond. Floating just beneath the surface, his face relaxed, his hands folded neatly on his stomach.

I leaned in close to the water. "Hello?"

He didn't respond. I waved my hand in front of his eyes. Still no response. A second figure appeared in the water to his right. Then a third. And a fourth. This continued until six forms bobbed gently just below the water's surface.

Each of them was different.

An Asian boy and a girl who looked like twins.

A dog that could have been a cross between a German shepherd and a poodle.

A little girl whose frowning face was adorned with large, round glasses and spotted with a galaxy of freckles.

And . . .

A face I couldn't help but recognize: Dixon Watts.

What was he doing in this deer's CPU?

And who were the others? They had to be connected to Shallix's plan. But how?

I stuck out my tongue and licked a streak of bird poop that had dried on the bark of a nearby tree. Geez. Even in a world made up of a bunch of 1s and 0s, I still did gross things.

I went back to Dixon, studying his pleasant features. How could a guy who looked so good sing so badly? The voice and the face were total mismatches. Like a dog that meowed or a goldfish that mooed.

As I stood there staring, a movement in the pond caught my eye. Something was floating up to the surface just to the right of Dixon.

Another person. Only this one lay facedown in the water.

I swallowed hard and reached toward it, trying to tamp down an intense feeling of dread.

As my finger broke the surface, the form rolled over. My gaze locked onto the figure's face, and a strangled cry burst from my throat.

It was me!

CHAPTER 8.0:

\ < value= [Let's Go Shopping] \ >

MY SCREAM ECHOED ACROSS SIX LANES of New York State Thruway as I opened my eyes. The Tick deer stared at me, unblinking.

"Seven Omicron," it wheezed in a barely audible whisper. Then it fell permanently silent.

"Sven!"

I looked up.

A short, round man stood over me holding an electrical cable. Despite his signature tangled nest of gray hair and paint-spattered clothes, it took me a few seconds to recognize him as Junkman Sam.

"Are you with us, Sven?" he asked. "Can you hear me?

I had to disconnect you. You went into convulsions. You were screaming. What happened in there?"

I blinked at him.

"Sven!" Will cried. "Say something! Come on, dude!"

"I . . . I think we're in trouble," I said once I found words.

Even in the darkness, I could see the color disappear from Will's face.

"Oh," he uttered shakily. "I was kind of hoping you'd say something a little less, you know . . . um, troubling."

Alicia squatted next to me. "What happened in there?"

"There were people in the pond!" I gasped. "And I was there too. And I was dead!"

"Are you okay, Sven?" Sam asked. "You're not making any sense."

"Nothing makes any sense! All I can tell you is I saw some people in the deer's mind."

"Who?" Alicia's eyes drilled into me.

"They basically looked like regular kids. Except for one who's, like, probably in his twenties. Oh, and there was a dog. And two kids who looked like twins. And, of course, I saw—"

"Did you see anything that can help us figure out who they are?" Sam interrupted. "Or something that can lead us to them?"

I shook my head.

Alicia fingered the blade of her knife pensively. "Wait. You said you were there too?"

A cold shiver ran through me. "Yeah. I was . . . dead."

"Do you think the six other people you saw were Ticks? Like you?"

"Maybe. Probably. I mean, they were inside the Tick deer's CPU. They must have something to do with everything that's going on, right?"

Alicia nodded slowly. "But we don't know who they are, where they are, or what they're going to do?"

"Not exactly," I replied.

"What do you mean?"

I stuffed my hands in my pockets. "I know where one is."

Will goggled at me. "Where?"

"Madison Square Garden."

"Wait." Alicia frowned at me. "Madison Square Garden. You mean it's—"

"Dixon Watts," I finished. "He was right there with the others."

"Come on, Sven! Seriously?" she countered. "Are you positive it was really Dix and not some other really attractive, super-talented guy?"

"Yes, I'm sure," I said emphatically.

Will chewed on his fingernails. "You're saying Dixon Watts really is a Tick?"

Sam jangled his keys. "I'd say there's only one way to find out."

The thing about Madison Square Garden is it's a really stupid name. I mean, the place is *round*. It's this big, *round* building in the middle of Manhattan. If it had been up to me, I would have built it with four corners. Then it would have been a square, and the name would fit a lot better. Still, dumb building names aside, New York was pretty amazing! I had never been there before, and my head practically spun as I looked up at the canyon of skyscrapers that surrounded us. How could they make buildings so tall? And how did they—

"Sven? Hello?"

I had been so fixated on taking in the sights that I had been completely oblivious to Alicia's attempts to talk to me.

"Huh?"

"I said, what's the plan?"

I stopped short. "Plan?"

"Yes, plan," she sighed. "You were supposed to come up with a plan for getting in to see Dix, remember?"

I looked to Will and Sam for support, but they just stared back at me expectantly.

"Right. The plan. Uh . . . well . . . um . . . you see . . ."

Alicia shook her head. "Yeah, figures."

"What's that supposed to mean?" I snapped.

From nowhere, that little voice in my head piped up again. *She's out to get you.*

"Geez, Sven. Chill out. I didn't mean anything."

I glowered at her. "So let me guess—you've come up with a brilliant idea."

She squared her shoulders. "As a matter of fact, I have. Let's go shopping."

Will looked around at the innumerable souvenir shops lining the street. "I don't think now's the time to pick up some I Heart New York T-shirts."

She grinned at him. "Yeah, I was thinking something a little different."

The "something different" Alicia had in mind was a hardware store a few blocks away. We arrived just as the owner opened for the day.

"Hi," Alicia said as she stepped into the small shop. "Where do you keep the sharp things?"

Ten minutes later, she dumped a basket-load of items on the counter. Half a dozen circular saw blades, ten packages of magnets, a lighter, eight bottles of superglue, wire cutters, a large spray bottle, duct tape, and a gallon of kerosene.

Sam paid for the assorted items and we hurried back toward Madison Square Garden, where the RV was parked.

Once Alicia had finished assembling her makeshift

weapons, we stepped out onto the street. Alicia's backpack bulged with six magnetic throwing stars made out of circular saw blades. And a "flamethrower," which was really nothing more than a lighter and the spray bottle she had picked up at the hardware store and filled with kerosene. Still, I wouldn't want to be standing at the wrong end of it.

Alicia assured us she used to make flamethrowers all the time back home in the Settlement, and she'd never lost even a single eyebrow. But that didn't make me feel any better. I wasn't sure which were more terrifying: the Ticks, or our own weapons.

CHAPTER 9.0:

\ < value= [Plan C] \ >

WE HAD WEAPONS. BUT WHAT WE DIDN'T have was a way into Madison Square Garden. Forget about getting past Dixon Watt's bodyguards, we couldn't even get by the skinny guy with the long, scraggly hair sitting at a plastic table underneath the awning that read SOUTH VIP ENTRANCE 31ST STREET. And even if we could get by him, the heavy steel gate he was guarding looked completely impenetrable.

I sighed. I wasn't sure I had ever felt *less* like a VIP than I did at that moment.

Nonetheless, that particular entrance seemed to be the least well-guarded way into the place. We had already ruled out the main entrances or either of the loading docks, since they were crawling with police officers—and none of us wanted to spend the next several years in jail.

So there we were, standing in front of a man who wore a windbreaker with SECURITY in big yellow letters on the back and EDDIE on the front, trying to trick him into letting us in. He took a big swig of coffee from a thermos. "Nope. I don't see none of your names on the list. Can't let you in."

"But I'm telling you," Alicia insisted. "We won the 'Meet Dixon Watts At Madison Square Garden' contest. Which means we're supposed to meet Dixon Watts. At Madison Square Garden. Which is here. So if you'll just let us in, that'd be great."

"I already checked the list. You ain't on it."

"Fine, *Eddie*," Alicia huffed. "But I'm sure Dix is not going to be happy when he doesn't get to meet his contest winners. And I'm going to make sure he hears that *you* were responsible."

Eddie's only response was a big yawn.

"Come on, guys." Alicia turned on her heel and strode away.

The rest of us followed her. Once we were out of the guy's sight, Alicia sighed.

"Well, that stinks. All right, plan B." She pulled the lighter and flamethrower out of her backpack.

"You can't just go around flamethrowing people!" Will cried.

She raised her eyebrows. "I'm only going to singe him a little."

Will pocketed the lighter. "No singeing people! Or broiling them. Or roasting them. Unless they're Ticks."

"That guy *might* be a Tick," she replied hopefully.

We frowned at her.

Her shoulders slumped. "Fine." She put the flamethrower away. "So, Sven? Did you end up figuring out a plan? Because obviously no one is behind mine."

I looked at the ground and watched a big black cockroach munch on a scrap of discarded bagel. "No."

I was suddenly immobilized by despair. Dixon was

our only lead. And we couldn't even come up with a way to get in the door.

I felt lower than that stupid cockroach.

Without thinking, I reached down, scooped the insect up, and raised it to my mouth.

"Dude! Gross!" Will cried. "I'm gonna totally barf!"

I stood there, mouth open, wriggling cockroach poised in front of my lips, as an idea popped into my head.

We watched from around the corner as Junkman Sam approached Eddie, got down on his hands and knees, and crawled under the man's table.

"Whoa! Hey!" Eddie cried, leaping up and knocking his chair over in the process. "What the heck, man! Get outta there!"

Sam gave the man an apologetic look. "Oh, sorry. I don't suppose you've seen a brown leather wallet, have you?"

"What? There ain't no wallet here. Get lost!"

"But I'm pretty sure I dropped it somewhere around

here," Sam replied, peering up at the guy from under the plastic tabletop.

Eddie squatted down next to Sam and gestured to the pavement under the table. "Use your eyes, man! There's no wallet under there! Now get outta here!"

Sam frowned at him. "You're sure?"

"Do you see a wallet?"

Sam scratched his head. "No, I guess I'll have to look elsewhere."

"Just get away from my table!" Eddie said.

Sam backed out on his hands and knees, straightened, and smiled at the man. He bowed slightly and walked back to Alicia, Will, and me so we could watch the action unfold.

Eddie righted his chair imperiously, plopped down onto it, and took a big gulp of coffee.

Before he could swallow, his bloodshot eyes nearly jumped out of his skull. Coffee shot from his mouth and nose, speckling the surface of his plastic table. As he gagged and spluttered, a big, black cockroach crawled out of his mouth, paused briefly under his nose, scuttled across his cheek, and vanished into his greasy hair.

It was the same cockroach I had dropped into his coffee while Sam was distracting him.

Squawking and batting at his head, he finally pulled the roach out of his hair, took one look at it, turned a really impressive shade of green, doubled over, and barfed.

While he was depositing the contents of his stomach all over the sidewalk, I walked up behind him and gingerly unclipped the security badge from his belt. He didn't even seem to notice.

I swiped his card through the card reader next to the gate. A soft metallic click let us know it was unlocked. I pulled it open and slipped inside, followed by my friends. By the time Eddie had stopped barfing, we had already swiped open another lock and pushed through a set of double glass doors to the interior of the building.

We found ourselves inside a hallway that extended at least a hundred feet in front of us. Banks of fluorescent lights gave the place a sterile feel. Even autographed posters from some of the world's biggest bands couldn't breathe life into the dreary space.

"Where do you think Dixon's dressing room is?" I whispered.

I got my answer in the form of a low rumble coming from the left. It sounded like a rusty buzz saw biting into a pile of human skulls.

We peeked around the corner to see two small mountains placed side by side in front of a door that bore a sign reading DIXON WATTS.

On closer inspection, I realized that they weren't mountains. They were just two of the largest men I had ever seen. And the rumbling sound was a deep laugh spilling out from a mouth containing two jumbled rows of missing and broken teeth.

Scars crisscrossed their faces and arms. Nearly every exposed inch of their skin, which looked as if it were about to split open under massively bulging muscles, was inked with elaborate tattoos. Even their shaved heads were adorned with swirls and symbols that wove in unsolvable knots around their skulls.

My feet went numb. "Are they Ticks?"

"Probably not," Alicia said with a note of disappointment. "If they were, they wouldn't have all those scars. Their repair systems would have healed them. Too bad. I so want to try out my flamethrower."

"Okay, so what do we do now?" Will breathed in a barely audible voice.

As always, Alicia had a plan. "Follow my lead. And stay cool."

Sam and I immediately glanced at Will.

"What?" Will insisted defensively. "I'm cool."

Alicia rounded the corner with a bold swagger. The rest of us shuffled along behind her with considerably less confidence.

CHAPTER 10.0:

\ < value= [You're a Poo] \ >

"HEY, GUYS!" ALICIA CALLED CHEERFULLY to the bodyguards. "We're here."

The man who was laughing abruptly stopped. "*Who's* here?"

"Us," Alicia replied. "Dix's opening act."

The two men scratched their shaved heads in unison.

The one on the right, who I noticed had the words LETHAL and WEAPON tattooed on the backs of his hands, was the first to respond. "Opening act? Mr. Watts didn't say anything about an opening act," he chirped in an improbably high voice.

"Yeah," rumbled the one on the left, who sported

a black skull-and-crossbones tattoo on his neck. "Mr. Watts doesn't need an opening act."

Alicia frowned at them. "Hold on! Are you telling me there's a mix-up with our booking? We're supposed to open for Dix tonight! We signed a contract!"

"I don't know anything about that," Lethal Weapon squeaked.

"You don't? Maybe we can just straighten it out with Dix, then?" She stepped forward. "If you'll just let us by . . ."

A hand the approximate size of Thor's hammer stopped her.

"Nobody sees Mr. Watts," the owner of the hand thundered.

Alicia shrugged. "Maybe you should take that up with our manager."

"Who's your manager?"

"Him." Alicia pointed at Sam, who seemed to physically shrink as he looked up at the bodyguard.

With a trembling hand, he waved. "Hi," he muttered softly.

"You don't look much like a manager," Lethal Weapon observed. "And they don't look much like an opening act. What do they do, anyway?"

Sam's face was blank for several seconds. Finally, he uttered, "Comedy. They do . . . stand-up comedy."

"Oh, yeah?" growled Skull-and-Crossbones. "I like jokes. They're funny. Go on. Tell us one." He pointed right at me.

I froze. I couldn't think of a single joke. Or gag. Or pun. Or funny story. Heck, under the circumstances, I would have been lucky to remember my own name.

Seconds ticked by. The men scowled at me. Thoughts swirled around in my head in a hopeless tangle.

Will cleared his throat. "Knock, knock."

The men aimed their intimidating gaze toward him. "Who's there?" they responded together.

"Europe."

"Europe who?"

"No, *you're* a poo."

Oh, no! Of all the jokes that Will could have told, he had to choose that one? I mean, sure, at least he'd come up with one. But that joke was lame when Sam's stupid jokebot told it to us yesterday. Now it was potentially fatal.

The bodyguards blinked.

"Get it?" Will coaxed. "Europe who? You're a poo? It's funny because I just called you . . . a . . . poop . . ."

I think that was the moment Will realized he had insulted our soon-to-be murderers because he suddenly turned very, very pale.

Skull-and-Crossbones began to tremble. His whole body shook with what I could only assume was homicidal rage.

Until . . .

He laughed. That same deep, bone-shattering laugh we had heard earlier.

A few seconds later, Lethal Weapon joined in—although the clueless look in his eyes suggested he wasn't exactly sure why.

Once he had caught his breath, the deep-voiced man smiled at us. "That was funny. You guys are funny. I guess you really are comedians. Because comedians are funny."

"So we can see Dix now?" Alicia asked.

The man's smile instantly disappeared. "Nobody sees Mr. Watts."

Alicia scowled, balling her fists and snapping into the taut combat stance I had seen her assume so many times over the past few days. No way she could even be thinking about taking these guys on!

"Alicia . . . ," I whispered.

But it was no use. She was laser-focused on her adversaries, ready to spring. It would have been admirable if it hadn't been so unbelievably stupid.

"It's okay, kids," Sam said. "If we can't see Mr. Watts, we can't see Mr. Watts. Let's go."

That managed to get through to Alicia. She rounded on Sam. "But . . . but we can't just—"

Sam put a hand on her shoulder, gave her a wink and uttered something in Russian. *"Sledovat' moyemu primeru."*

The hint of a smile played across Alicia's lips. "Okay, you're right. We should go."

And just like that, she turned and strode away from the bodyguards.

I set off after Alicia with one final look over my shoulder at Dix's dressing room door. We had been so close!

But before we had taken half a dozen steps, Junkman Sam turned back to face the men. "But . . . as long as I'm here . . . can I ask you two a question?"

The men looked at each other and gave Sam a nod.

"Great. You see, I've been dying to get my first tattoo. But I just can't decide what to get. And since you two look like experts, I thought you could offer some advice?"

The bodyguards' eyes lit up.

"Tattoos are *awesome*!" squeaked Lethal Weapon.

"Exactly," Sam confirmed. "That's why I want to make sure I get a really good one."

He pulled out a marker and rolled up his sleeve. With a few quick strokes, he sketched a heart on his forearm.

"What do you think?"

"That stinks!" exclaimed the low-pitched one, snatching Sam's marker. "What you need is something like this."

He crossed out the heart and drew what was either

meant to be a grinning skull with a bunch of snot dripping out of its nose hole or a deformed octopus.

As I watched the bodyguards use Sam as their personal sketch pad, I felt a tap on my shoulder. Alicia held her finger to her lips and nodded toward Dix's dressing room door.

We crept down the corridor, opened the door, and slipped inside.

What we found there was truly horrific.

CHAPTER 11.0:
\ < value= [I Want to Poke My Ears Out] \ >

"BABE, YOU ARE MY SCRAMBLED EGGS! I love you and your bacon legs!"

Dixon Watts stood in front of a mirror in his dressing room, warming up his voice. Unfortunately, no amount of warm-up would make him sound like anything other than a tone-deaf bull elephant.

I stuck my fingers in my ears, but it didn't help. It was as if his voice tapped straight into my brain and scrambled it like a two-hundred-horsepower eggbeater.

I glanced at Alicia and Will, who stared, starry-eyed, at Dix.

"Do re mi fa—"

The teen pop idol stopped short when he noticed us standing behind him. "Oh, hi. Just leave them over there." He gestured toward a table at the side of the room and turned his attention back to his reflection.

We stood there for a few seconds as the auditory torture continued. Finally, when he paused to comb his eyebrows, I pulled my fingers from my ears and spoke up.

"Um . . . put what over where?"

"The D&D's," he replied.

I scratched my head. "What?"

He spun around, his face looking a lot less handsome thanks to the angry scowl that spread across it. "The D&D's! My manager always sends a list of my requirements ahead of time. It specified that I am to have in my dressing room, available for my consumption before every show, a bowl filled with two and a half pounds of blue D&D's! And I don't see any blue D&D's in my dressing room!"

"What are blue D&D's?" I asked, shrinking away. He stood a whole head taller than me and his muscular arms strained at his tight black T-shirt. Jeez, why couldn't I have been the good-looking, tall, muscular Tick rather than the weird Tick who ate garbage?

Dix sighed and rolled his eyes. "As you *should* know, D&D's are M&M's that have had the *M*s scrubbed off and have *D*s painted on in their place. *D* for Dixon. *M*s are stupid letters. And 'blue' means blue. I won't eat any of those other colors. They stick to my vocal cords. Now do you have my D&D's or what?"

I looked at Alicia and Will for support, but they were too starstruck to do anything but grin.

"Oh. Uh . . . no," I answered. "We're here about something else."

"Did you bring me a pet monkey?" Dix demanded.

"Uh, no monkey. Sorry," I told him.

His mouth curved into an angry frown. "No monkey? Then why. Are. You. Here?"

I blinked at him as I tried to figure out the best way to tell the world's most popular musical artist that he was really a Tick. "Um, you see, we wanted to talk to you. About you."

He cocked his head at us for a moment, then forced

himself to smile. "Oh, I see. You're reporters here for an interview. Fine. Normally, my manager handles the press. But since she's out, I guess I can talk to you. But next time I want a monkey."

Pet monkeys? D&D's? Reporters? Seriously? How can someone who's been a star for only a month be this out of touch with reality?

I took a deep breath and let it out slowly. "Maybe you should sit down, Dix."

He scrunched up his neatly combed eyebrows. After a moment's hesitation, he sat on a couch.

"Okay," I continued. "I'm not exactly sure how to tell you this, so I'm just going to tell you. You're a—"

I was interrupted by the dressing room door bursting open. An old lady shuffled into the room, her silver hair tied into a tight bun, her neatly pressed red pantsuit hanging loosely off her narrow shoulders. She carried a bowl of blue candy.

Dix leapt up. "Oh! Hi, Roz! You have the D&D's! Awesome! You're the best manager ever!"

The lady smiled at him, her jumbled teeth as gray as

tombstones. "I will always take care of you, Dixon." She scuffed across the room and placed the bowl on the table. "And who are your . . . friends?"

Dix grinned. "They're reporters!" he enthused.

"Are they?" Roz replied flatly, slowly turning to take Alicia, Will, and me in with her wet, milky eyes. She pursed her lips. "Funny how I wasn't informed of any reporters coming today."

There was something about this woman that made me uneasy. My stomach felt hollow—the same kind of sensation I'd get just after Brandon Marks did something to humiliate me in front of the whole school. I swallowed down the lump of panic that was forming in my throat.

The arrival of the creepy manager was enough to snap Alicia and Will out of their Dix-induced stupor.

Alicia took a few seconds to shake the fog out of her head before speaking. "Yeah, we're not reporters. We're here about the day of reckoning. *Srok rasplaty*. And we're going to stop it."

At the sound of the Russian words, the woman flinched. But she immediately recovered and smiled mildly at us. "Dix, be a sweetie and step into the bathroom for a few minutes. I'd like to have a word with these charming young people."

"But I don't need to go to the bathroom," Dix informed her.

Roz fixed him with her gaze.

Dix seemed to shrink. "Okay, I guess I do need to go to the bathroom," he muttered, slinking into the bathroom and shutting the door.

"He's a sweet boy. And such a talent," Roz said. "I try to shield him from things that might upset him."

"Like the fact he's a Tick?" I shot back. "Like the fact he's part of a plot to destroy the entire human race?"

Roz looked at me thoughtfully. "Well, yes. Also bloodshed. The poor dear has such a weak stomach. He hates it when things get . . . *messy*."

Alicia scoffed at her. "You're threatening us? Please. We've taken out tougher Ticks than you, old lady!"

"Seriously?" Will whispered to Alicia. "Do you have to antagonize her?"

Instead of responding, the woman just kept smiling

with those crooked, gray teeth, her milky eyes boring into us.

A shudder coursed through me as I realized she didn't blink. *Just like Dr. Shallix!*

The old lady slipped off her jacket and carefully hung it over the back of a chair. She turned back to face us in a crisp white blouse.

Alicia hoisted the backpack off her shoulders without taking her eyes off the woman. Her hand dipped inside and reemerged holding the flamethrower.

That's when things got, well . . . disturbing.

The old woman's pristine white shirt began throbbing. Dozens of little . . . *things* poked at her shirt from the inside. It almost looked like fingers were jabbing at the garment.

Thirty long, thin tentacles exploded from under the woman's shirt. Each was about ten feet long and tipped with a gross yellow fingernail, which gave them the overall appearance of fingers that had been stretched out to an absurd length. Only, fingers weren't usually covered by suckers that looked like they belonged on an octopus.

Will leapt back toward the dressing room door faster than I'd ever seen him move before. He wrenched at the knob.

But before he was able to open the door more than a few inches, one of the woman's appendages shot out in a flesh-colored blur and slammed it shut.

"No, no, my sweet children," she cooed gently. "You cannot leave now. I haven't had a chance to kill you yet."

CHAPTER 12.0:

\ < value= [Octogranny Doesn't Eat Fire] \ >

THE ROOM WAS ALIVE WITH TENTACLES. They flailed and whipped around the old lady, their fingernails hungrily seeking human flesh.

"So you know about *srok rasplaty*," Roz said. "Very clever, children. But there's nothing you can do to stop it. Once I dispose of your bodies, Dixon will go onstage as planned. The whole world will be listening. All his earlier songs were merely softening up the humans' weak brains. Tonight, when they hear the debut of his latest masterpiece, they will be completely under his influence!"

"Eat fire, Octogranny!" Alicia growled. She raised the flamethrower toward Roz. Her eyes gleamed ferociously as she reached into her pocket. Then she froze. "Hold on. Where's my lighter?"

Will cleared his throat and held up the lighter he had confiscated from her earlier. "Sorry, I meant to give this back."

He tossed the lighter toward Alicia, but one of Roz's tentacles darted out and snatched it from the air midflight. A sharp hiss of escaping butane signaled the lighter's demise. Roz dropped its blue plastic carcass on the floor.

"Oh, did I break it? I'm sorry, sweetie," Roz simpered. "But you may as well come to terms with reality. You might have defeated Dr. Manson Shallix, but you will not escape me."

She read the surprised expressions on our faces and laughed. "Of course I know what happened to him. Each Omicron unit has an overseer. And each overseer works as part of a team to ensure our plan moves forward in the event of unforeseen complications. I was aware the very moment Dr. Shallix was deactivated. I could *feel* him go offline."

Overseers? The implications made my fingers tingle

with panic. If there were six more Ticks to track down, that meant there were six more overseers that we were going to have to get through first!

A pair of Roz's tentacles wrapped themselves around my waist. They felt like steel cables. No matter how hard I struggled, they didn't budge.

The sound of something clattering to the floor drew my attention to Alicia. The flamethrower had been torn from her grasp, the fluid inside seeping uselessly into the carpet. At least half a dozen of Roz's limbs encircled Alicia, pinning her arms to her sides and lifting her a foot off the ground.

I turned to Will just in time to see Roz immobilize him, too.

"Let go of us!" Alicia snarled.

Roz shook her head slowly. "Stop struggling, dear. You'll only make this more painful than it needs to be."

One of Roz's tentacles reached out and caressed my cheek with its thick, discolored nail. "So you are Seven Omicron. Dr. Shallix cared for you so very much. It's a shame you ended up disappointing him."

"Don't call me that! I'm *Sven*, not Seven!"

"You are Seven Omicron," she tittered. "You represent the epitome of Synthetic development. As does my dear Dix, of course. Or, as he is properly designated, *Six Omicron*."

At the mention of his name, Dixon called out from the bathroom. "What did you say, Roz? Can I come out now?"

"Nothing!" the woman barked. She paused and added in a voice dripping with honey, "Just a little longer, Dixon, sweetie. You stay in there. I've almost finished with these . . . reporters."

Of course! Dixon had no idea he was a Tick. And Roz wanted to keep it that way. If he saw her for who she really was, he might be too freaked-out to sing.

"Dixon!" I shouted. "Oh, wow! Your pet monkey is here! And he's so cute!"

Roz's eyes grew wide. In an instant, every single one of her tentacles had retracted and disappeared back under her blouse. Will, Alicia, and I tumbled to the floor.

By the time Dixon had emerged from the bathroom,

Roz looked every bit the frail old *human* lady. If it hadn't been for the fact her shirt was in tatters, you'd never have known anything was wrong. But Dix was way too focused on searching for a domesticated primate to notice.

"Dixon, sweetheart," Roz chirped. "You should go back into the bathroom until I've finished with our visitors."

"But my pet monkey!" the pop star replied with an imperious scowl. "Where is it? I was told there'd be a pet monkey!" Dix began turning over couch cushions and emptying dresser drawers.

"Dixon, sweetheart," Roz said soothingly. "Perhaps you can go back into the bathroom. . . ."

"No! I! Want! My! Monkey! *Now!*" Dix replied.

"Dixon, please be reasonable," Roz pleaded. "Tonight is the most important performance of your life. We don't want you stressing your vocal cords, now, do we?"

"There won't *be* a performance if I don't get a pet monkey this instant!" Dixon snarled.

The fury on Roz's face slowly transformed into something else. Fear. "But you . . . you *have* to perform tonight.

Your show is being simulcast on nearly every television and radio station on Earth. It will be the biggest musical event in history. The *whole world* will be listening."

Dix glared at her.

"Dixon, honey, not performing would be—waaghhh!"

Whatever she was about to say dissolved into a startled yelp as a round, jag-toothed steel blade buried itself in the side of her head.

Alicia had taken advantage of Roz's distraction to heave one of her magnetic throwing stars at the Tick's head.

"Chew on that, *sweetheart*," Alicia taunted.

Roz's body jerked rigid, and she spoke in a mechanical monotone. "Physical breach. This unit is under assault. Damage assessment in progress."

The tentacles she had hidden from Dix reemerged and gingerly reached up toward her head like a cluster of long, boneless fingers. Whenever they'd get too close to the magnets affixed to the blade, they'd recoil as if in pain.

I could see the skin and bone around Roz's injury

struggling to heal. Her emergency repair system was kicking in. If the blade hadn't been magnetized, Roz probably would have already shrugged off Alicia's attack as nothing more than a minor inconvenience.

But for Ticks like Roz—and me—magnets were the last thing you'd want anywhere near you. I should know. My face had been nearly ripped off by an electromagnet in science class. These weren't nearly as strong, but they were enough to keep Roz's wound from healing.

"Condition red. Defense mode activated," Roz intoned. Her tentacles shot out violently, whirling in a deadly storm around her.

Dixon looked on in disbelief, a creak escaping his lips. It was probably the most musical thing that had ever come out of him. He finally stopped creaking and switched to making actual words. "What the heck is happening to her?!"

"Your manager is a Tick," Alicia replied, her voice dripping with venom. "And so are you."

Dixon shook his head. "She's a . . . I'm a . . . *what*?"

Alicia ducked under a tentacle, which passed close

enough to ruffle her black hair. "Can we please discuss this when she's not trying to kill me?"

"She's not just trying to kill *you*!" Will corrected, as a tentacle barely missed him. Instead, it slammed into a stack of mail, sending it cascading to the floor. "Do something!"

"Regeneration systems f-f-failing," Roz announced flatly. "System shutdown i-i-i-imminent." Her tentacles drooped and hung limply by her sides.

"There. Happy?" Alicia replied.

The saw blade clattered to the floor as the side of her head collapsed like a rubber Halloween mask. All that was left of her above the shoulders was a metallic box connected by a thick silver cable to her torso.

Roz's arms reached up suddenly to the place where her human head should have been. She shook her fist at us a second before she slumped to the floor.

CHAPTER 13.0:
\ < value= [A Slip of the Tongue] \ >

THE ROOM FELL SILENT.

Dixon sat heavily on the couch. "I'm totally losing it, right? This is all some sort of hallucination. Somebody slap me."

I turned to Alicia and Will. If they weren't going to do it . . .

I stepped forward and slapped Dix's face. I might have been a little overzealous about it. Oops.

"Ow! Hey!" the teen idol yelped.

"Sorry. But you did ask," I told him, trying my best to smother my grin. "You're not hallucinating, though.

She's a Tick. A Synthetic life-form designed to pass as human."

"But-but-but-but . . . I don't understand," Dix stammered. "It doesn't make sense. This can't be happening."

Alicia sat down next to him and explained everything. The Soviet robotics program that gave birth to the Synthetic race. The secret war Synthetics were waging against humanity.

Dixon leapt up from the couch. "You're completely loony! Either that or this is some kind of really stupid joke!" He looked at me. "How can you expect me to believe this?"

"Because I'm one too," I replied. "And if we don't do something to stop the people who created us, everyone on the planet is doomed."

The pop star's eyebrows shot up. But then a scowl appeared on his face. "No!" he roared. "I don't believe you! You killed Roz! I won't let you do the same to me!"

His muscular arm shot out in a right hook, his fist arcing toward the person closest to him. Unfortunately for Dix, that person was Alicia. She ducked his punch easily and sprang back up, delivering an uppercut to the bottom of Dix's jaw.

A *clack* filled the room as Dixon's teeth snapped together under the force of Alicia's blow. Something tumbled through the air and landed on the toe of my shoe.

"Ahhh!" Dixon screamed. "My ongue! I bi off my ongue!"

It took me a few seconds to realize what an "ongue" was. But looking at the pink object on my shoe and watching Dixon dance around the room holding his hands over his mouth, I put the pieces together and realized . . . Dix had bitten off a piece of his tongue!

I extended my foot toward him, trying not to let the chunk of tongue fall to the floor. "Um . . . here."

Dix regarded the piece of tongue like it was the most disgusting thing he had ever seen—which it probably was. He slowly reached his hand out and picked up the fleshy object that used to be firmly attached to him.

"Look what you did!" he cried through his fingers. "How am I going to ing with half a ongue! I cang ing like iff."

"Oh, uh . . . sorry," Alicia muttered. "Reflex. But it doesn't look like a lot of tongue. You probably had more than you needed, anyway."

He looked like he was about to respond when he froze. The piece of Dixon's tongue flattened itself out in his palm, then squeezed its ends together, inching up to his wrist like an inchworm. It reached his shoulder, at which point it made a detour to the right and squirmed across his chest.

"That's so nasty," Will remarked, scooping up a handful of D&D's and arranging them in neat rows on the table.

When the piece of tongue reached Dixon's chin, it forced its way into his mouth.

"Aahhhhhh!" Dix screamed. "Wha happening?" His eyes goggled wildly in his head. "My ongue! It'th . . . it'th . . . it's . . . it's . . . *better.*"

He poked his now-healed tongue out and studied it in the mirror. It looked as good as new.

"Don't worry," I assured him. I had seen far too many weird things over the past few days to freak out over a crawling piece of tongue. "It's a Tick thing. The same thing happened with my arm when it came off."

"Y-your arm? What do you mean?"

"I told you," I explained. "You and I are both Synthetics. So was your manager. I found out I . . . wasn't human when I lost my arm in a bike accident and it reattached itself. Now we're trying to stop the Ticks from exterminating everyone on Earth."

"And you're part of it." Alicia fixed him with an icy gaze. Now that she saw what he really was, the starstruck spell she'd been under was broken.

Dix flinched at the menace in Alicia's expression. "You're saying I'm part of a plan to hurt people? That's insane! All I want to do is write my music and sing."

"Your singing is part of the problem," I told him. "It has an effect on humans. Makes them act strangely. Do things they normally wouldn't do. But to me, everything you sing sounds . . . well, awful."

A hurt look spread across his face. "You don't know what you're talking about! Everyone loves my music!"

"Yeah, humans love your music," I replied. "Because

you've been programmed to make music that humans love. But it's really just a way to control them."

"You're . . . you're saying my music isn't good?" Dix growled, his fists clenched tight. "The song I was going to premier tonight? It's my best yet! Listen to this."

"No! Wait," I cried. "Don't si—"

"Ooooh yeah, girl, you make me cry; I love you so, I want to die. Our love can never be undone; it burns as brightly as the sun. I will never stop the fight; to exterminate the human blight."

As soon as Dix started singing, my friends' faces went blank. Then, without warning, their hands closed over each other's throats.

CHAPTER 14.0:

\ < value= [I Spill Some D&D's] \ >

"STOP!" I YELLED. "STOP SINGING, DIX! Look what you're doing!"

But he was too focused on his caterwauling to hear me.

Aside from the fact that it featured what were quite possibly the worst lyrics ever written, Dixon's song had to be stopped—before Alicia and Will killed each other.

I picked up the first thing that caught my eye—the big, heavy glass bowl full of D&D's—lifted it over my head, and brought it down right onto the singer's cranium. He was halfway through an *Oooh* when, with an explosion of glass and blue candy, the bowl hit its mark.

The horrific sounds pouring out of Dixon's food hole fell silent as he crumpled, unconscious, to the floor.

Will and Alicia froze. They slowly lowered their hands to their sides and blinked.

"Wh-what happened?" Will croaked. "Why does my neck hurt?"

"Dixon's new song made you want to kill each other," I told her. "If I hadn't stopped him, you probably would have."

Will rubbed his neck. "Wait. I was trying to kill Alicia?" He cleared his throat and added sheepishly, "Sorry about that, Alicia. My bad."

"Forget it." Alicia ran her fingers along her black braids before stooping down to rummage through her backpack. Pulling out a roll of duct tape, she bent over Dixon's unconscious form, gagged him, and taped his hands behind his back. "Imagine what would have happened if he had performed tonight."

Will opened and closed the bathroom door. "Everyone in Madison Square Garden would have killed each other."

"Not just Madison Square Garden," I corrected. More like the whole world. You heard his manager. This show was going to be broadcast live on practically every TV and radio station on the planet. If the entire population of Earth reacted the same way you two just did . . ."

I couldn't bring myself to finish the thought.

The silence hung heavily in the air.

Until Dixon stirred. "Mmmnnngggg," he moaned. "Hmmnggg mnngggg mumphfff!"

Alicia squatted down next to Dix. "Listen to me carefully, Dixon. I don't want to have to deactivate you. But I will if you try to sing again. Understand?" She kicked what remained of Roz to punctuate her point.

Dix's eyes widened with fear. He nodded.

"I'm going to take the duct tape off your mouth so I can ask you a few questions," she continued. "But if I hear anything musical come out of you, it's the last thing you'll ever do. You get me?"

She yanked the tape off Dixon's mouth.

"Yeowww!" he cried. "Wh-what's going on?"

"I'm asking the questions," Alicia snapped. "We

already know your mission. Your singing can control human minds. If you went onstage tonight, you would have started the most deadly riot the world has ever seen. What I want to know is who else is involved besides you and Roz."

Dix shook his head. "I don't know what you mean. I just like to sing."

"Don't lie to me!" Alicia snapped.

"I have no idea what you're talking about! This was supposed to be the biggest day of my career! Now Roz is dead and you're telling me I'm some kind of . . . of . . . *flea*!"

"Tick," Will corrected.

"Whatever!" Dixon wailed. "I just want things to go back to normal!"

"Dix," I said. "Listen to me. Nothing is ever going to be normal again. Everything you thought you knew about your life is a lie. I know that's tough to hear. I didn't want to hear it myself. But I understand who . . . *what* I really am now. And, yeah, it stinks. But there's no way I'm going to let the people who created us win. So we need you to tell us everything you know, okay?"

Dix nodded.

The only problem was, everything Dix knew was not very much at all. His parents adopted him when he was an infant. Roz showed up when Dix was only five, telling his mom and dad he had "an extraordinary gift" and it would be a "crime against humanity" not to share it with the world. For the next decade, Roz worked intensively with Dixon, until she decided the time was right to "unleash his talent."

That was about a month ago. Since then, Dixon Watts had skyrocketed to greater fame in a shorter time than any other performer in history. He'd also become the most spoiled, overprivileged performer in history, at least if his pet monkey tantrum was anything to go by.

"That's it?" Alicia demanded.

Dixon trembled. "I swear I don't know anything else. I just thought I was a normal kid. Well, other than being extraordinarily talented, I mean."

I rolled my eyes. "Ohh-kay, right. Listen, we need to get you out of here. The Ticks must already know about Roz, so we don't have long. Let's go."

"I'm going to free your hands," Alicia told him, using her knife to cut the duct tape from his wrists. "Don't make me regret it. Because I guarantee you'll regret it more."

He glanced at his former manager and shuddered. He may have been a full head taller than Alicia, but at that moment, he seemed to shrink to half her size. "Okay," he squeaked. "But where are we going? I'm not sure I want to go with you."

"Trust me," I explained. "You want to come with us. With Roz deactivated, the Ticks will be sending someone—or something—else. They already know your mission is compromised. Which means they'll want to deactivate you."

He flinched at the word. "Deactivate?"

"He means they'll kill you," Alicia said matter-of-factly. "So unless you want to end up like her"—she nodded toward Roz—"you'll come with us."

His head bobbed in a series of quick little nods. "Okay, fine," he said in a small voice. He stooped down to pick up the mail scattered all over the floor.

"What are you doing?" I asked.

"Today's fan mail," he explained. "You don't expect me to leave my fan mail behind, do you? I read it every day. Sometimes people send me presents."

Alicia sighed. "Whatever. Take your stupid fan mail. Just be quick about it. If more Ticks get here before we leave, we'll never get out of here alive."

CHAPTER 15.0:

\ < value= [Smells Kinda Fishy to Me] \ >

"WHAT DO WE DO NOW?" WILL ASKED AS soon as we climbed into Sam's parked RV. "I mean, it's great that we stopped Dix from singing tonight and all, but aren't there still five more Ticks we have to worry about?"

I nodded somberly. "Yeah. And they could be anywhere. Anyone have any ideas?"

"Well . . ." Sam, who was now largely covered by the bodyguards' sketched tattoo designs, held up a cable.

I stopped him. "I mean ideas that *don't* involve cutting open the back of my neck and hooking me up to something that might fry my brain."

Sam fell silent and shrugged.

Alicia shook her head.

Will tapped his fingers on the wall, his lips pressed into a thin line.

"So we have no clues at all?" I sighed.

My question was met with blank stares.

Except from Dix. He was completely absorbed in tearing through his fan mail. "Ooh, candy!" he cried, stuffing his mouth with chocolate truffles. "I love when they send me candy!"

I watched as he ripped open envelope after envelope, box after box, chirping in delight at every single gift, love letter, and piece of fan art.

Until he came to one package in particular. He frowned at the brown cardboard box before sliding open a window and heaving it out.

"What was wrong with that one?" I asked.

"Nothing," he said casually as he ripped open another letter.

Alicia threw herself into the passenger seat and thumped her fist against the dashboard. "Darn it! What now? Where are those other Ticks? There has to be some way to find them!"

Sam shook his head. "I don't know. But there's no point in sticking around here. The Ticks will know we have Dixon. We should stay on the move."

He started the RV and pulled onto Thirty-Third Street.

As I watched Madison Square Garden fall away behind us, I kept replaying the image of Dix throwing that package out the window. Why would he do that?

When we had traveled about three blocks, it hit me.

"Stop!" I shouted.

Sam slowed the RV to a halt.

I ran for the door. "Wait here. I'll be right back."

Without waiting for a response, I jumped down to the sidewalk and sprinted back to where we had parked.

After a minute or two of frantic searching, I found the package underneath a parked minivan. I dropped to my stomach and retrieved it. As I stood up, a dark form streaked just over my head. But before my eyes could lock onto it, it was gone.

"What was that all about?" Will asked as I climbed into the RV.

"This." I held the box up for everyone to see.

Dix's eyes grew wide. He shifted in his seat. The envelope he was holding slipped through his fingers and fell to the floor.

I stepped toward him. "You didn't want us to see this, did you? What's in it? Why were you so eager to get rid of it?"

"What are you talking about, Sven?" Alicia asked.

"I've never seen anyone so excited to get mail," I explained. "So what is it about this box that made him want to ditch it?"

Sam raised one bushy eyebrow. "I'm guessing you have an idea?"

I nodded. "I think Dixon hasn't been completely honest with us. And I bet this package is going to tell us why."

Dixon shook his head. "Trust me, you don't want to open that!"

Alicia scoffed. "Sven, open it."

I tore the cardboard flaps open and was immediately met with a smell so horrific that it nearly made my knees buckle—a stench somewhere between the beach at low tide and the inside of a garbage can stuffed with rotten meat.

I recoiled and dropped the box onto the dining table. It landed with a slightly moist *thump*. I held my breath and peeked inside.

Nestled in the box was a dead fish about eight inches long. Written on a tag attached to its tail were the words: *You sing even worse than this smells!*

"Seriously, Sven? This was your big 'aha' moment?" Alicia said. "It's a fish."

"And it's stinking up my RV!" Sam added.

I scratched my head. "Why would someone send you a dead fish?"

"Who sent it?" Will added.

Dixon sighed. "Ivy. Her name is Ivy. And she seems to get a real kick out of telling me how much she hates my singing. I recognized the handwriting on the box, so I tossed it out."

“What do you mean?” I asked.

“Three days ago, she sent me a bag full of chopped onions with note that said, ‘Your voice makes me cry more than these.’ Two days ago, it was a lump of stinky cheese that said, ‘Like a fine cheese, your singing gets smellier with age.’ And yesterday, she sent me a can of fart powder.”

“What did the note with that one say?” Will scratched his chin.

“It said, ‘I’ve met farts that sounded better than you.’”

Somebody laughed. It might have been me.

“Sorry to disappoint you, Sven,” Dix mumbled. “Your big lead is nothing more than hate mail.”

I was about to step outside to find a garbage can for the fish when it hit me. “No, it’s not. This fish is going to lead us to a Tick!”

CHAPTER 16.0:

\< value= [We Get Lunch] \>

"WHAT ARE YOU TALKING ABOUT?" WILL argued. "It's just some hate mail."

I nodded enthusiastically. "Exactly!"

"And?" Alicia prompted.

I smiled. "Whoever sent this must be a Tick! If they had been human, they would have loved Dix's singing, right? Every human does! So all we have to do is find the person who sent this fish to him!"

Alicia's eyebrows rose a fraction of an inch. "That's pretty good," she said with just a hint of admiration in her voice. "So where did it come from?"

I looked on the box and my heart sank. "There's

no return address here. All I can find is a postmark. Look."

"Colorado Springs," she read aloud, straining against the smell. "Fine, so we have a name and a city. But there must be a million people in Colorado Springs."

"Actually," Will corrected, "there are about four hundred fifty-six thousand."

We stared at him.

He shrugged. "What? So I happen to know the population of the top fifty cities in the US. Is that a crime?"

Alicia snorted. "It might as well be a million. How are we ever going to find one Tick hiding in a city with four hundred fifty thousand residents?"

"We don't have to find her," Dix said suddenly.

"Why not?" Will asked.

"Because she'll find me. Now, who has a phone?"

Alicia handed him her phone.

After a quick Google search, Dix dialed and pressed the phone to his ear. "Hi there. Am I speaking with the Happy Hog Barbecue Emporium in Colorado Springs? Great. This is Eugene Rosebottom, Dixon Watts's personal bodyguard. I'm calling because Mr. Watts is going to be making an unannounced visit to Colorado Springs and wants to stop by the Happy Hog for lunch tomorrow. We'd like to reserve a table at noon."

He waited for a reply.

"No, this isn't a hoax," he continued. "Mr. Watts specifically mentioned your establishment and asked me to contact you. Can you make a table available for Mr. Watts or should he take his business elsewhere?"

Another pause.

"Thank you. And I'm sure I don't need to tell you, but we'd appreciate it if you didn't make it widely known that we'll be there. We'd hate to have a huge crowd show up at your restaurant."

After a few more seconds, Dixon hung up.

Will furrowed his brow. "Wait, if the plan was to spread word that we were coming so we'd have a chance of finding Ivy, why'd you tell them you didn't want anybody to know?"

Dix smiled. "When was the last time you met anyone who could keep a secret?"

* * *

The Happy Hog Barbecue Emporium was not a fine dining establishment. Normally, it would be the type of place I would have gone out of my way to avoid. But after the twenty-seven-hour journey to Colorado Springs—punctuated by nothing but nondescript highway rest areas that all seemed to serve variations on the same semi-edible food—my mouth was practically watering just looking at the restaurant's dirty gray concrete exterior. Neon signs glowed from every window. Not that it was easy to see the place at all. It was largely obscured by the thousands of people milling about in the parking lot.

Every single one of them was there to see Dix.

My mind reeled at the thought. He was a Tick programmed to destroy the human race, just like me. But instead of being shunned by everyone he met because he did really gross things, he was adored by pretty much the whole planet.

I sighed and slouched in my seat. I was *Seven* Omicron. He was *Six* Omicron. We were separated by just one model number. Yet it felt like we couldn't be further apart. He had everything. Fame. Money. Success. He was tall. He was muscular. Handsome. Popular. I had nothing. I *was* nothing.

Hot flames of jealousy licked at the inside of my chest. *It's so unfair! Why couldn't I be the popular one? Why couldn't I be him?*

In an instant, envy transformed into rage. And a tiny, cold voice rang out from the dark recesses of my mind. *Kill them. Do it. Do it now.*

"Sven?" Alicia said gingerly.

Sitting bolt upright, I fixed her with a wild stare. "*What?*" I snapped furiously. My entire body tensed. For the briefest moment, I was overcome by an almost uncontrollable urge to punch her in the face.

"Whoa," she replied with an almost imperceptible flinch. "Easy, Sven. I just wanted to see if you're coming with us. You okay?"

I noticed the others looking at me with concern.

The anger drained away as quickly and inexplicably as it had arrived. "Uh, yeah," I muttered. "Sorry. I'm okay."

I got up shakily from my seat and flashed my friends what was probably a pretty unconvincing smile.

What the heck was happening? These moments of fury coming out of nowhere. That voice in my head saying things I didn't even want to think about. It didn't feel like me. Except that it kind of did. When the anger took over, it felt like it was spreading from a solid ball of radioactive rage right in the center of my body.

What if that's who I really was? What if when you got right down to it, all that was inside of me was a deep preprogrammed loathing of every human on the planet?

Will's stomach rumbled loudly, shaking me out of my miserable thoughts. "I've never been so happy to not be a vegetarian in my entire life! I'm starving!"

The sound of Will being so . . . well, *Will* helped shake me out of my mood.

We stepped out of the dingy RV and found ourselves under an immense blue sky, with rugged mountains jutting up on the horizon.

The fans, who were packed into the parking lot, must have expected the great Dixon Watts to arrive in some sort of fancy limo or helicopter or decked-out tour bus instead of a rusted crud bucket of an RV. Because it took a full twelve seconds before the screams started.

"It's him! It's Dixon!"

The roar that followed seemed to distort the air around us with its volume. My eardrums were on the verge of tearing themselves to shreds.

Dix shouted in my ear to make himself heard over the crowd. "Sucks, right? I can't go out for a walk without being mobbed."

I rolled my eyes. *Oh, boo-hoo! Try spending a few days in my shoes!*

Still, I thought, as the noise of the crowd washed over us, he did have a point. The starstruck fans were a little overwhelming. "Hold on a second!" I yelled. "I'm going to go on ahead. I'll meet you inside the restaurant."

I pushed through the throng of screaming fanatics, trying to avoid getting trampled. Eventually, I made it to the front door of the barbecue joint and pushed my way inside.

"We're eating in here?" Will asked as he sat down in front of a massive slab of ribs and licked his lips hungrily. "I mean, I'm not complaining, but this place is definitely lacking in the ambience department."

He was right about that. We were seated at a plastic folding table in the middle of a storage room. Steel shelving units crammed with cans, bottles, and boxes lined the walls. Hard-edged shadows morphed and wobbled with the gentle swaying of a single naked lightbulb hanging from the ceiling.

"I think it's perfect!" Dix smiled at me. "Thanks for setting this up, Sven."

"I just figured we could use a little peace and quiet while we ate. And the owner of the place was happy to help."

As if on cue, the latch on the room's steel door clunked loudly and a large gray-bearded man wearing a red bandana on his head entered. "Hi, everyone. I'm Earl, owner of the Happy Hog. But everyone just calls me Porkbutt. Can't say I love the nickname. But it's mine. Anyhoo, Mr. Watts, sorry to seat you here in the storage room. But when yer friend Sven said you wanted privacy, it was all I could think of. If there's anything else I can bring you, just say the word."

"Thanks, Porkbutt," Alicia replied with a warm smile. She gestured toward the metric ton of ribs, brisket, chicken wings, corn bread, baked beans, collard greens, coleslaw, pulled pork, and mashed potatoes spread out in front of us. "I'd say we're good."

The man left us alone with our mountain of meat.

Dixon belched. "This is great! It's the first time I've had a meal outside of a dressing room or tour bus in ages. I think—"

Whatever Dix was thinking was interrupted by something exploding against his forehead.

CHAPTER 17.0:

\ < value= [Something's Rotten in the State of Colorado] \ >

THE ROOM FILLED WITH THE SMELL OF sulfur.

"We're under attack!" Alicia cried, rolling out of her chair and dropping into a combat stance.

Sam peered around the room anxiously. "I don't see anything. Maybe it was just—"

Another projectile burst across Dixon's chest.

It was white and yellow. And incredibly stinky. It . . . it was . . . a rotten egg.

Just as I came to that realization, two more eggs found their mark—the face of the world's most popular singer.

"Where are they coming from?" Will asked.

Another egg struck home.

"You like that, Dixon?" The taunt was delivered in a high-pitched voice. "Now you know how I feel when I listen to you sing. Only, these eggs? They're a lot less rotten than your songs!"

"It's . . . it's . . . it's . . . *you*!" Dixon said, his words dripping with dread. "Ivy."

The voice tittered. "Aw, that's so sweet. I guess that means you got my presents."

"I don't see anyone here! Where are you?" Alicia snarled. "Show yourself!"

"I'm right in front of you," the voice answered.

I squinted in the direction of the voice, but I couldn't see anyone . . . until I realized I was staring at a little girl. Even though I could see her, I couldn't *see her* see her. I knew she was standing there. And that she was short and skinny. Beyond that, I couldn't really say what she looked like. It was like my eyes just seemed to, well . . . slide off her and focus on something else.

I tried to make out the color of her eyes, but I found myself looking at a box of bread crumbs on the shelf next to her instead. When I tried to see what her hair looked like, my eyeballs seemed to skip right over her and come to rest on a bucket and mop propped by the side of the door.

Another egg splatted against Dix's shoulder.

"Can you *please* stop throwing eggs at me?" Dix begged.

After a pause, Ivy replied. "Sure. I'll stop. As long as you promise to stop singing. Forever."

"You really don't like his singing, huh?" I asked her.

"Are you kidding? He sounds like when my third foster dad would use the bathroom after eating too many nachos. Only worse. He sounds like . . . like . . ."

"Like an old man sitting in the park hawking up a big mouthful of phlegm?" I suggested.

"Yes! Exactly!" the girl chirped. "And then spitting it right into your earhole! Thank goodness *someone* gets it!"

I stifled a laugh.

"But how did you get in here without us seeing you?" Will scratched his head. "There's only one door. And no windows."

"Yet here I am, carrot top." Ivy tossed a rotten egg into

the air with her left hand and caught it deftly between her right finger and thumb. "I'm sneaky, like a ninja. You chumps never even noticed me! I was standing here for ten minutes before the egg-stravaganza! Get it?"

Alicia groaned. "So, how old are you, anyway? Like five? Six?"

"No! I'm ten! Almost. In eight months."

The longer Ivy talked, the clearer I could see her. She had curly blond hair. And, I realized as they came into focus, pale blue eyes that were magnified by a large pair of glasses with round frames. A smattering of freckles dotted her face. Her clothes were drab and shapeless. She was the type of girl you'd pass on the street a million times and never even notice she was there. Still, as my eyes finally focused on her, I knew that I *had* seen her before.

"I saw her in the pond when I interfaced with that Synthetic deer. She must be an Omicron!"

She turned to face me and sneered. "What are you talking about, jerkface? My name is Ivy Grissom, not Anne Omi-whatever the snot you said."

"It's a pleasure to meet you, Ivy Grissom. My name is

Sam." Junkman Sam smiled and extended his hand, which the girl pointedly ignored. "These are my friends Alicia, Will, and Sven. You already know Dixon Watts, I guess."

"I wish I didn't," she mumbled with a frown.

Sam squatted down so his face was at the same level as Ivy's. "Aren't you a little young to be out here by yourself, throwing rotten eggs at people? Where are your parents?"

Ivy, who had tossed the egg into the air once more, missed the catch. The egg splatted on Sam's shoe.

"I don't have parents!" she spat. "I have *foster* parents! Believe me, it's not the same thing!"

"Do they know you're here?" Sam continued gently. "I'm sure they're worried about you if you snuck out on your own."

"First of all," Ivy snapped, "stop talking to me like I'm a baby. I told you I'm almost ten. Second, they're not worried about me. They don't even know I'm gone. And if they did, they probably wouldn't care anyway."

"I'm sure that's not true," Sam replied.

"It is true! I'm on my fifth set of foster parents in the last three years! None of them cared about me! They all kept shipping me back like I was some kind of defective toy they didn't want anymore. And then they'd shuffle me to some other family who would keep me for a while and then get rid of me. All because I ran away from home once or twice! Or maybe a few dozen times. But still!"

Alicia pulled a chair around and sat down in front of her. "Why do you keep running away from home?"

"Why?" Ivy screeched. "*Why?* Why do birds sing? Why do fish swim?"

I thought she meant those as rhetorical questions, but she glared at us, waiting for an answer.

"Um," Will ventured. "Because that's what their instincts tell them to do?"

"No, dummy!" Ivy scowled at him. "It's because they're freaking good at it!"

"Um . . . so . . . you're saying you run away from home because you're good at it?" I asked.

She puffed out her chest. "Not good. I'm awesome! Never been caught once sneaking out of a house. I can be practically invisible when I want to be. Doesn't matter if they lock the door, turn on the burglar alarm, whatever.

No one can catch me! Except Bing. He always seems to track me down before I can get very far."

I shrugged. "Who's Bing?"

"The social worker who's in charge of placing me with foster families. He's always looking at me with his fishy eyes and saying things like 'Now, now, Ivy, we mustn't run away. You're such a very special little girl.' *Blah, blah, blah!*"

"And where are you trying to run away *to*?" Sam tilted his head at her inquiringly.

Without saying a word, Ivy walked out of the storage room and stopped at the front window of the now-empty Happy Hog. "There." She pointed at a mountain that loomed in the distance. "That's where I want to go. Don't ask me why. It just . . . I don't know . . . calls to me. I have these super-realistic dreams about the mountain, and I . . . I just feel like I have to go there."

"But why?" I asked. "What's there?"

"That right there's the Cheyenne Mountain Complex," a voice said behind us. It belonged to Porkbutt. He joined us at the window and stroked his long beard thoughtfully. "Home of the US Strategic Command's Missile Warning System. The place is built right into the mountain, protected by two thousand feet of granite. If some poor fool of a country launches a nuclear attack against us, that facility can direct our entire nuclear arsenal to retaliate. Kaaaa-*boom*! And then it's buh-bye, world!"

CHAPTER 18.0:

\ < value= [I Give Ivy the ~~Bad~~ Good News] \ >

THE ROOM SPUN AROUND ME AS PORKBUTT'S words sank in. Whatever Ivy was programmed to do, I felt pretty sure it involved the Cheyenne Mountain Complex. Why else would she be so obsessed with the place?

Alicia caught my eye. Judging by the grim look on her face, she had come to the same conclusion. "Her mission has something to do with the military installation in that mountain."

"But what is it?" Will asked, nervously shredding a paper napkin.

Alicia shrugged. "Whatever it is, I'm going to guess

there's a good chance it involves the nukes Porkbutt was talking about. All I know is, I'm going to make sure she doesn't do it."

I pulled her away from the window so Ivy couldn't hear us. "You're not talking about killing her. She's just a little girl."

Her steely eyes met mine. "She's a Tick, Sven. And she's been programmed to kill us all."

"Yeah," I snapped. "So is Dix. And I don't hear you talking about killing him."

"That's because we already stopped him from performing at Madison Square Garden," she replied. "And as long as he's with us, we can make sure he doesn't do any singing. And if he's not singing, he's harmless."

"Oh, right." I snorted. "Yeah, I'll bet *that's* the reason."

She glared at me. "What's that supposed to mean?"

"It means I'm sure his being tall and good-looking and wearing a tight T-shirt that shows off his muscles has *nothing at all* to do with it," I answered sarcastically.

Her face flushed pink. Whether it was with embarrassment or anger, I wasn't sure.

"Uh-huh." She rolled her eyes. "Jealous much, Sven?"

Without warning, a hot surge of rage overtook me. My heart pounded, and my pulse thundered in my ears.

Once again, an urgent voice rang out, delivering a message that felt as if it had burrowed its way up from some deep, uncharted part of my brain.

Kill her. Do it. Kill them all.

"Sven? Sven, you okay?" Alicia's voice was shaded with concern.

The anger slipped away like sand escaping between my fingers. "Wh-what?"

"I was asking what you thought we should do about Ivy," she said. "But you were just staring at me with this weird look on your face. Is something wrong?"

"No, no . . . nothing's wrong," I lied. "I was just thinking about . . . you know, junk and stuff."

She looked like she didn't believe me. "Ohh-kay. If you say so. But what do you think about Ivy? We can't risk her carrying out her mission."

"No, we can't," I agreed. "That's why I say we take her with us. If we put a few hundred miles between ourselves and the mountain, that ought to keep her out of trouble."

"We don't even know her, Sven," Alicia argued. "Who knows if we can trust her?"

"We didn't know Dix, and you didn't seem to have any reservations about taking him along," I countered.

Again, her cheeks reddened. "Will you give it a rest, Sven? Fine. You want to take her, we'll take her. But you're telling her she's a Tick, not me."

Alicia strode away and sat down heavily on a chair. Folding her arms over her chest, she glowered back at me.

I walked back to the window wondering how in the world I was going to get Ivy to believe she wasn't a real human. It took having my arm fall off and reattach itself before I even started to realize there was anything going on with me. And Dixon wasn't convinced until the tip of his tongue leapt into his mouth to repair itself. How could I possibly get her to understand?

"Hey, Ivy," I said hesitantly. "Can I . . . talk to you for a minute?"

* * *

When I had finished telling Ivy that she was a Tick who was designed to wipe out the entire human race, she stared into my face for a full ten seconds without saying a word. Finally, she spoke.

"Oh my gosh! You're saying I'm . . . I'm . . . some kind of . . . killer android?"

I nodded gravely. "I know it's not easy to hear."

Ivy stared at her hands as if she was seeing them for the first time. "I'm not really human? That's . . . *AWESOME*! So do I have all kinds of, like, androidy superpowers?" She fixed her eyes on a nearby red-and-white checked tablecloth. "Can I burn stuff with my eyes? Come on, *burn*!"

"No, you're thinking of Superman," I told her. "You don't have heat vision. But wait—why do you think this is awesome? You're not actually human. Doesn't that bother you?"

She laughed. "Seriously? What's so great about being human? My whole life I thought I was human, and nobody even knew I existed. Half the time my foster parents would call me down to dinner when I was already sitting at the table. It was like I was the invisible girl or something. But now? If I have the whole world's fate in my hands, people will *have* to pay attention to me! I'll be more famous than Dixon Watts! *Ivy, the girl who ruled the world!* Has a great ring to it, right? So how am I going to destroy the world, anyway?"

"Well, first of all, we're not sure. Second of all, you're not going to destroy the world. That's why we tracked you down. So we could stop you."

"Hold on!" She frowned at me. "You're telling me I finally have something that'll make people notice me and I have to just shut up and sit down?"

I chewed on my lip. "Yeah. But, believe me, there are worse things than having no one notice you."

"Oh, yeah?" she sniffed. "Like what?"

"Like having *everyone* notice you . . . but for all the wrong reasons," I explained. "Like me. My whole life I would have done anything to be invisible. Even if it was just for a day. Because what people noticed about me were all the things I wish no one noticed at all."

"For example?" she prodded.

I sighed. "For example, licking garbage can lids. Eating the mold off yogurt that's two years past its expiration date. Just yesterday, I almost ate a cockroach."

She narrowed her eyes at me. "That's seriously nasty!"

I shrugged. "So maybe being invisible isn't all that bad?"

She chewed on her thoughts for a few seconds. "Maybe."

"But you know what?" I added. "If you come with us, you can help save the world, instead of destroying it. And I'd say that's a better way to get noticed, wouldn't you?"

"Maybe," she repeated. "I'll tell you what. I'll come with you, but if I don't like the whole saving-the-world thing, I want you to drop me off back here so I can go ahead and destroy it. Deal?"

She extended her hand.

"If it involves you destroying the world, it doesn't seem like a very good deal to me," I told her.

She waggled her hand at me. "Take it or leave it."

"Fine," I sighed. In the end, it wouldn't really matter what I agreed to. If we failed in stopping the other four

Ticks that were out there, they'd probably beat Ivy to it.

"So listen," I told her. "We need to get out of here before your overseer finds us."

"Aw, geez. I'm afraid it's too late for that," a way-too-happy-sounding voice piped up behind us. "But don't worry. I promise I'll kill you quick!"

CHAPTER 19.0:

\ < value= [No, It's Not Fun] \ >

"OH HI, BING," IVY SAID.

I turned around to find Ivy peering up at a slim middle-aged man dressed in a sweater vest that looked like a unicorn had thrown up on it. His sandy hair dipped limply onto his large forehead, and a neatly trimmed mustache adorned his upper lip.

"Now, Ivy," Bing chirped. "We've talked about this before. You're a very special girl. You can't just go traipsing around whenever you feel like it. No-siree Bob!"

Ivy's shoulders sagged. "I guess you're going to take me home?"

Bing laughed. "No, silly-billy! Tonight you get to go to the mountain. Just like you've always wanted."

"You mean I can really go there?" A broad grin spread across Ivy's face. Her lips fell into a confused frown. "Wait. How do you know about the mountain? I never told you about that. It was—"

"In your dreams? Of course I know about that, cupcake." Bing sat down and leaned in close to Ivy. "Sheeesh. I know exactly what you dream about, Ivy. You dream about the mountain. About pushing that button. The one that's going to usher in a new Synthetic age. It's why you were created. Now, just as soon as I take care of your new little friends here, we'll go to the mountain. We could take a picnic lunch! Wouldn't that be fun? Yay!"

"You're not taking her anywhere," Alicia growled, pulling a magnetic throwing star from her backpack.

Bing got one look at her weapon and his smile evaporated. "Oh, no! I—I didn't mean it! Please just don't hurt me! Please! I'm sorry!"

Great sobs wracked his body, and he retreated to the corner and slumped to the floor.

Alicia looked confused. "Well, okay, then. Next time you, um, decide to mess with humans, you'd better—"

"Just kidding!" Bing cried, leaping to his feet with a giggle. "You actually thought I thought you were scary! Hee hee! But you wanna see something *really scary*?"

Without waiting for an answer, Bing . . . *yawned*?

I braced myself, certain that some horror was about to be unleashed. But the only horror in sight was a set of brownish molars and Bing's yellow-coated tongue. Which were gross, obviously, but hardly terrifying.

His yawn grew, his mouth stretching to inhuman dimensions, complete with squishy sound effects, until something seemed to wriggle up his throat and onto his tongue. It was a . . . a . . .

"Ugh, nasty!" Will gasped. "A centipede!"

"No, it's a scorpion, dummy," Ivy told him.

The truth is, they were both right. What was crawling out of Bing's mouth had the body of a centipede and the arched, stinger-tipped tail of a scorpion. A . . . a . . . scorpipede! About six inches long, the disgusting creature squirmed over Bing's chin and scurried down his body until its many feet were resting firmly on the scuffed wood floor of the Happy Hog.

In an instant, another emerged from Bing's mouth, followed by another and another, until dozens of the horrific things swarmed across the floorboards. Their hard, pointed legs clicked audibly as they moved. It sounded like the chattering of a million tiny teeth.

Once the last of the creatures left Bing's mouth, the man's empty skin crumpled to the floor.

"We are the Bing Collective," the creatures said in unison, a chorus hundreds of voices strong. "A multitude as one. Isn't that fun? Yay! The one you knew as Bing was merely our exterior flesh sac!"

One look at the scorpipedes' shiny black exoskeletons was nearly enough to cause my barbecue lunch to make a reappearance.

"It's so nice that you've met your brothers, Ivy," the Bing Collective chittered. "Five Omicron with her big brothers, Six and Seven. It's like a family reunion!"

Ivy swallowed hard. "Bing? Have you always been a

big man-shaped skin pouch stuffed full of a bunch of gross scorpion-centipede things?"

"Well, it sounds pretty unflattering when you put it that way, but essentially yes. We've been watching you, Ivy. We've been following you. Making sure you were safe. Moving you to a new foster home every time you did something to make your family suspicious. You see, because of a glitch in your latency algorithm, you kept trying to carry out your mission early. But no matter how much we truly wanted to let you, we had to wait until the time was right. And now that Dixon Watts—Six Omicron—has failed, it's your turn!"

The scorpipedes squiggled excitedly around the room.

Will kinda freaked when one scuttled over his foot.

"Eww! Eww! Eww!" he shrieked. "This is so gross!"

He stamped wildly with his feet until—*squish!*

The sharp, metallic smell of sizzling circuits reached my nose.

Will lifted his foot. A flattened member of the Bing Collective was stuck to the sole of his sneaker.

Alicia's lips pulled back into a malicious grin. "Good thinking, Will. Hey, Sven. Whaddya say we stomp these bugs?"

With a *crunch*, she crushed a scorpipede under her boot. I followed her lead, slamming my foot down on one of the creatures that happened to be scuttling by.

"Yeah!" Will taunted. "Rule number one: Never bring a centipede to a foot fight!"

Alicia, Dix, and I all looked at him. "What?" we said together.

Will shrugged. "Forget it. Just get them!"

The Bing Collective quickly retreated and crowded around the empty skin that used to house them, a glinting, pulsing mass of nastiness.

"What's wrong? Don't like getting squished?" Alicia laughed.

But the Bing Collective laughed louder. "You actually think you're hurting us? We are too numerous to be defeated. Sure, some may fall, but you can't get us all. Hey, that rhymes! Fun!"

The Bing Collective surged forward, scrabbling over

the floor and surrounding us. A burning pain exploded in my ankle. I hitched up the leg of my pants and peered at a red dot that looked way too small to have caused the agony radiating along every nerve ending.

"Ouch!" I yelled.

"Hee hee," the Bing Collective giggled. "Yes, a single sting hurts, doesn't it? But a hundred stings? Ooh, that's a killer!"

CHAPTER 20.0:

\ < value= [We Get Mobbed] \ >

"THERE ARE JUST TOO MANY OF THEM," Sam called, trying to catch his breath.

We were all tired. Alicia, Will, Dix, Sam, and I had been stomping like crazy for the past ten minutes. But those scorpipedes were quick. For every one we squashed, we missed a bunch more.

The Bing Collective was right. There were more scorpipedes than we could ever hope to defeat. Just as I introduced one to the sole of my sneaker, I felt the stinger of another sear into the flesh of my calf.

Dix reached over and swiped one of the creatures

off my shoulder. "Sven, we need more feet. There're too many of them!"

Ivy, who had been standing to the side, watching the scene unfold, wore a look of helpless confusion.

"Ivy!" I called. "Help! Please help us!"

She blinked at me, gave a curt nod, and raised her foot. But then uncertainty clouded her features. She stood with one foot in the air for several seconds before lowering it slowly to the floor.

"Excellent, Ivy," the Bing Collective crowed. "I knew you could never hurt us. You're just a big lovey-dovey cuddlepuss. Now execute your prime directive like a good girl. Go to the Cheyenne Mountain Complex and rain fiery nuclear destruction down on the human race!"

Ivy froze in place, her head swiveling from me to the horde of scorpipedes and back to me.

"I—I . . . I don't know," Ivy replied.

"What do you mean, you don't know?" The Bing Collective rippled all around us, their stingers poised to strike. "You've always wanted this, you silly goose!"

The girl scratched her curly blond head. "Well, yes . . ."

"Exactly! So go! Do what you were always meant to do!"

"Ivy?" I pleaded one last time.

She looked at me for only a second before she turned on her heel and strode out the restaurant's front door.

"Ivy, no!" I called after her. "No!"

The creatures laughed as one. Without warning, they crawled back toward the rumpled skin on the floor, freeing us from the thousands of legs that had been crawling over our bodies. "You see? You can't change her programming. She was designed for stealth, for entering even the most secure facilities, bypassing the most advanced security systems, evading detection—all so she could, when the time was right, gain access to the Complex and launch a preemptive strike against all of humanity."

"But won't the nuclear war kill you, too?" I reasoned desperately.

"We hope so!" An excited ripple went through the Bing Collective. "We'd be gosh-darn proud to make that sacrifice for the greater good! But ask us about the good news for you."

Will's voice shook as he spoke. "What's the good news for us?"

"We're so glad you asked," it chirruped back. "We're going to let you live to witness the Synthetics' grand victory. Which, unless we are very much mistaken, should happen just as soon as Ivy infiltrates the Complex and initiates the launch codes. Yay!"

It laughed, flooding the air with hundreds of squeals of delight.

The creatures' collective laugh withered as the front door of the restaurant burst off its hinges and fell to the floor with a crash. Hundreds of screaming Dixon Watts fans streamed into the Happy Hog.

"Where is it?" a large man wearing a Dixon Watts T-shirt several sizes too small for him bellowed as he lurched toward the kitchen.

"It's mine!" screamed a teenage girl with blue hair tied into a long ponytail. "I'm his biggest fan! I deserve it!"

Whatever the "*it*" was they were arguing about must

have been pretty awesome. They were so desperate, they paid no heed whatsoever to the disgusting Ticks under their feet.

"Hey, wait!" the Bing Collective wailed, its voice barely reaching my ears. "You're stepping on us!"

Flattened against the restaurant's walls, our little party did its best to evade the seething crowd of Dixon fans. Dix, himself, had thrown a barbecue-stained napkin over his head to prevent them from tearing him limb from limb in their rabid enthusiasm. The Bing Collective's screams grew fainter and less frequent as the mindless army of Dixon Watts fans stomped across the floorboards, crunching arthropod bodies underfoot.

"Come on, Sven! Let's go!" Alicia grabbed the collar of my shirt and yanked me toward her. "We have to stop Ivy!"

We struggled against the incoming tide of humanity. My feet threatened to slip out from under me as they skidded on the slick layer of slimy crushed Bing Collective that covered the floor. By the time we emerged into the bright sunshine I felt like I had just gone ten rounds with an octopus wearing boxing gloves.

"What was with the stampede?" Alicia asked.

"Let's worry about that later. First we need to find Ivy!" Sam instructed. "Spread out, everyone! She can't have gotten far!"

There were still tons of people milling around the parking lot, and they all closed in on us in their effort to get inside the Happy Hog. And that was a serious problem. Because it was tough enough seeing Ivy when she was standing right in front of you in an empty room. But in a crowd like this? It was hopeless!

"Dix!" I yelled as an idea popped into my head. "Head that way! Toward the corner of the parking lot. If you can draw the crowd away, maybe we'll have a better shot at finding Ivy!"

Dix nodded at me and leapt onto the hood of a car with effortless grace. "Hey, everyone," he screamed, ripping the sauce-stained napkin from his face.

He jumped down from the car and started pushing through the crowd to the far corner of the hot black asphalt. His mass of fans started after him. Alicia, Will, Sam, and I barely managed to avoid being swept away with the crowd. But as the last of the screaming admirers pushed by us, we found ourselves alone in the middle of the lot.

My eyes scanned the area, looking for any sign of Ivy. Will and I ran around, urgently calling Ivy's name. But there was no point. She was nowhere to be found.

This was bad. If we didn't find her, we were all going to end up vaporized. Everyone on Earth would be wiped out. I thought about my mom and dad back in Schenectady. What would happen to them? Would they be instantly incinerated? Or would the radiation get them slowly. I wished there was a way I could warn them. But even if I could get word to them, they'd still be overwhelmed by the Ticks as soon as they came out of hiding.

My eyes stung with tears as I thought about being so far away from them. Only they wouldn't be missing me at all, because Fake Sven was filling in for me. I was still bitter about the fact my parents couldn't tell the difference between me and the fake me. He had a face where his butt should've been! Why did that two-faced knockoff Sven get to hang out with Mom and Dad doing fun stuff while I was out here looking for a snarky little girl whose biggest ambition in life was to blow up the world?

"Sven? Will?" Sam's voice tore me from my somber thoughts. "Any sign of her?"

I wiped my eyes with the back of my hand and shook my head.

"That's not good," he replied quietly. "She could be nearly at the Complex by now. If we don't find her . . ."

He didn't have to finish the thought. We knew exactly what would happen if we didn't find her.

We'd all be dead.

CHAPTER 21.0:

\ < value= [I Get a Little Sister] \ >

"WE HAVE TO GET TO THE RV!" SAM CRIED. "The only chance we have is to get to the Cheyenne Mountain Complex before Ivy does. We can warn the guards she's coming. If we're not already too late."

Will chimed in eagerly. "Good idea! If the whole place is on high alert, there's no way she'll be able to get in!"

I nodded, but I had my doubts. I thought about how my eyes couldn't seem to fix on Ivy back in the storage room. And Bing said she was specifically designed to sneak into the most secure facilities. Even if we did manage to get to the Complex before Ivy, it might not do any good.

"What about Dixon?" I asked, nodding toward the crowd of fans on the other side of the lot.

"Leave him," Sam answered. "There's no time. We can pick him up later."

If there is a later, I thought glumly.

We sprinted to the RV, Sam jiggling and huffing and puffing as he struggled to keep up with us.

Will reached the door first. He tugged on it. "Locked. Hurry, Sam!"

"Coming." Sam wheezed, joining us with a set of keys in his hand. He unlocked the door and pulled it open. "Let's go."

We stepped into the motor home.

"Where are we going?" a voice rang out.

Ivy's voice.

As my eyes adjusted to the dim light, I could just make out Ivy, sitting with her feet up on the dining table and gnawing on a rib. She licked her fingers and dropped the stripped bone into a foam takeout container.

"Ivy?" I gaped. "What are you doing here?"

"Eating, duh. That Porkbutt guy makes some good ribs."

"But I thought . . . we thought . . . didn't you . . . ?" Will cocked his head at her. "I thought you were going to the mountain! To, like, totally blow up the world!"

The girl picked her teeth with a shard of rib bone. "Yeah, I decided not to. But, geez! Did you see Bing? I had no idea he was a big, gross bag of bugs. I guess he was a Sympathetic, huh? Like me?"

"*Syn*thetic," I corrected. "But not like you. Dixon, you, and I are the most advanced models they've built. Bing definitely wasn't. We've been designed to pass as completely human. That's not going to happen if you're stuffed full of centipedes."

Sam sat down next to Ivy. "So were you responsible for the stampede back in the restaurant?"

Ivy beamed. "Yep! I figured five pairs of feet wouldn't be enough to stomp those Bing things in there. So I told the crowd that there was a golden ticket hidden somewhere in the Happy Hog and whoever found it would get to hang out with Dix backstage at his next show."

"Wait," Alicia interjected. "Why didn't you go

through with your mission? That thing in there—the Bing whatever—said getting inside that mountain is what you want most in the whole world."

Ivy's cheeks reddened in a blush. "Yeah, that's what I thought too. But I guess we were both wrong. Turns out the thing I wanted most of all . . ." She fixed her eyes on me. They sparkled excitedly. ". . . was a brother. And now I have *two*!"

"So how do we figure out where to go next?" Dix asked once we had rescued him from his adoring fans.

"I have an idea," Sam said.

"No cables!" I snapped.

Sam's shoulders slumped in disappointment. "Fine."

"Look, we can figure this out," I insisted. "Think about it: We know that Ivy is really Five Omicron. Dixon is Six, and I'm Seven. And now that Ivy isn't going to destroy the world, the next Tick in line will be up to bat. If the order holds, that should be Four Omicron."

"So we know he's Four Omicron, but where are we going to find him?" Will asked nervously.

Ivy angled her head at him. "Maybe the next one's a girl!"

"You're both wrong," I corrected, playing the scene from the Tick deer's CPU over again in my memory. "Four Omicron is a dog."

Alicia raised her eyebrows. "You're sure about that?"

"A German shepherd, I think," I added. "Or maybe a poodle. Or a little of both?"

Alicia snorted. "Well, that narrows it down a lot. Thanks, Sven."

"Hey, watch it, jerkface!" Ivy snapped. "That's my big bro you're talking to. Go ahead, Sven," she cooed sweetly, grinning up at me. "Don't listen to her."

I felt myself blush. "Uh . . . um . . . Ivy, I'm not *really* your brother, you know."

"Sure you are!" she chirped. "You heard Bing. You and Dixon and I are a family. But you're my favorite," she added in a loud whisper while she beamed at me.

We're about as much a family as a bunch of cars that came off the same assembly line. I started to tell her as much when I caught her bright eyes gleaming at me. So I bit my tongue and gave her a feeble smile. "Ohh-kay. So anyway, anybody have any ideas where to start looking?"

Will shrugged. "I mean, dogs are *everywhere*. My cousins Steve, Danielle, and Peter have three dogs. And you know what they named them? Steve, Danielle, and Peter. They gave them their own names! Which is so stupid because nobody knows who they're talking to when they call—"

"Uh, Will?" Alicia interrupted. "Not now."

"Right," Will said, scratching the back of his neck as he stared at his feet. "Sorry."

"Maybe we could start calling animal shelters and ask if they have any poodle–German shepherd mixes," Sam suggested.

I nodded. "Well, that's an idea. Anyone know how many animal shelters there are in the country?"

"Too many." Dixon shook his head. "It's not going to work. Trust me. I spent who knows how many hours searching animal shelters online looking for a monkey. And you're assuming this dog is actually up for adoption, which it probably isn't."

I sighed. Dix was right. We weren't going to find Four Omicron by looking in a shelter. I could think of only one thing to do. "Fine. Sam, you want to hook me up to something, hook me up to something. Grab your cables and let's get this over with."

CHAPTER 22.0:

\ < value= [The Runt of the Litter] \ >

"I'M NOT ENTIRELY SURE THIS IS GOING to work," Sam mused, after we had returned to the Happy Hog. He squinted at a tiny silver box dangling at the end of a minuscule cable that stuck out of the gooey remains of a squashed scorpipede. "It's too small. I don't think I can connect you to this, Sven."

"So wait. That's it? You're saying there's nothing we can do to find Four Omicron?"

I looked to each of the others in turn. No one met my eye.

"Well, I'm not willing to accept that!" I continued. I marched over to Bing's discarded flesh sac. Ignoring how utterly disgusting it was, I picked it up and shook it in Sam's direction. It felt like a heavy leather blanket. "Maybe you can hook me up to this!"

Alicia shook her head. "Sven, I think that's just an empty skin. It's not—"

The words caught in her throat.

"What?" I asked.

I followed her gaze to the flesh sac. As I watched, a scorpipede no bigger than my thumb wriggled out of the mouth and scrabbled onto my wrist. I froze.

"Hey, man. Who's shaking the flesh sac?" it asked in a tiny voice.

Dix jabbed a finger at the creature. "Stomp it, Sven! Kill it!"

"Whoa, whoa, whoa," the thing cried. "Hold on. There's no reason to do that! It's cool, man!"

I hesitated.

Alicia glared at me. "What are you waiting for? Mash that foul thing!"

The scorpipede swiveled to face her. "Hey! You're no prize pig yourself! Besides, what'd I ever do to you?"

"Oh, I don't know," Will replied. "How about try to sting us all to death?"

"Not me, man. I never stung anyone."

"Really?" I snorted. "Because it sure felt like we were getting stung."

The scorpipede spat out a tiny laugh. "Don't look at me. That was the Bing Collective. I don't even have a stinger."

I took a closer look at the creature. It was right. "Hold on, you're saying you're not part of the Bing Collective?"

"Not me. I'm just plain old Bing 808. You can call me 808 for short. The Bing Collective would never let someone like me into their little club. Ever since we were created they've always teased me, called me the runt of the litter. And when they all formed their neural link, they left me out. Eight hundred eight of us all together, and I'm the only one who didn't get an invitation. They made me live down in the little toe of the flesh sac too. Not a nice neighborhood, believe me. Stinky. Cramped. And whenever they'd go out stinging, they'd be like, 'You stay here, 808. Guard the little toe in case any big, bad foot fungus comes around.' Then they'd laugh. Jerks. Honestly, though, I think they were just jealous of my awesomeness. Hey, what happened to those guys, anyway?"

I gestured at the slimy remains of the Bing Collective smeared all over the floor of the Happy Hog.

"Oh," 808 said. "Well, can't say they didn't deserve it. And, bonus: I guess I have the whole flesh sac to myself now. Nasal passages, here I come!"

Dix squinted at the creature. "So . . . you don't want to kill us?"

"Should I? You seem cool to me, man. And the way I see it, I owe you one for squashing those Bing Collective guys. They were making my life seriously miserable."

He owed us one? A tiny ember of hope sprang up in my mind. "Hey, no problem. Glad we could help. Maybe you could . . . do us a little favor in return?"

808 scratched his little insectoid head with one of his legs. "I'll try."

"I don't suppose you know where we could find Four Omicron, do you?"

"Four Omicron? Hmmm, let me check the network.

Hold on a second." The little scorpipede went silent for a few moments, then he spoke. "Okay. Got him."

Alicia's eyes lit up. "You found him? Awesome! Where is he?"

"44.5263 degrees north latitude; 109.0565 degrees west longitude," 808 told her.

"And where exactly is that?" Will asked.

"I'll tell you what," he answered. "Take me with you and I'll show you. I've always wanted to see the world."

Let's put it this way: I would almost have preferred spending the last six hours listening to Dix sing over having to spend six hours cooped up in the RV with Ivy being all sweet and doe-eyed and constantly referring to me as her brother. Don't get me wrong. I had nothing against her personally. Well, nothing other than the fact that she was a cranky little bundle of annoyingness. But what was worse was how uncomfortable it made me whenever she used the word "*brother.*" I still didn't think being manufactured in the same line of synthesized life-forms actually made us siblings. And it was . . . well, *stressful.* I mean,

I had never been a big brother before. What was I supposed to do when she beamed up at me with her big blue eyes? Did I have to hug her? Or tease her? Pull her hair?

And then there was the whole embarrassment factor. Every time Ivy called me her "big brother-wother," I could feel everyone's eyes bore into me. Plus, I was starting to get the feeling she and Alicia didn't like each other very much.

"Don't tell me what I can and can't do!" Ivy shook a tiny fist at Alicia.

Alicia sighed. "All I said was, 'You can't be serious about wanting to destroy the planet.'"

"See?" Ivy crowed triumphantly. "You said I *can't* be serious! I can be serious about whatever I want! Watch! I seriously think you're ugly!"

Her eyebrows arced downward, and she squinted, steely eyed, at Alicia.

"See how serious I'm being?" she said with a frown.

Alicia shook her head and muttered a phrase that sounded a lot like *rain in the grass*, but was probably something much worse.

"Big brother!" Ivy cried. "Alicia's being mean to me!"

"I'm about to get a lot meaner," Alicia countered through clenched teeth.

Just as Ivy opened her mouth to respond, the RV's tires crunched over loose gravel, and we slowed to a stop.

"Are we there?" I asked Sam.

"Not yet," 808 called from the dashboard. "Still about three hours to go." He'd been perched up there since we left Colorado Springs, a living, talking GPS guiding us to our destination.

Ivy yawned. "So why are we stopping?"

"I need some sleep," Sam replied. "It's late, and we're not going to be doing ourselves any favors if I fall asleep behind the wheel. Get some rest, everyone. We'll continue first thing in the morning."

We all agreed with Sam's plan, spreading out on various surfaces in the motor home—except for 808, who shimmied eagerly into the nose of the Bing flesh sac.

I grabbed a spot at the end of the couch and leaned my head against the fake-wood-paneled cabinets. It was far from comfortable, but I didn't care. I probably wouldn't be able to sleep anyway, with all the worries buzzing around in my head. After all, the longer it took us to get to Four Omicron, the more likely it was we'd be too late.

CHAPTER 23.0:

\ < value= [I Kill My Friends] \ >

I OPENED MY EYES AND FOUND MYSELF at the verge of a cliff that fell away to a broad expanse of jagged rocks about a thousand feet below. Just glancing over the edge made my stomach turn. Yet I felt an uncontrollable urge to step out into the empty air.

"Don't do it, Sven!" a voice called from behind me.

I turned to see Alicia, Will, and Sam standing a dozen feet from me, peering at me with pleading eyes.

"Come on, Sven," Will begged. "Get away from the cliff. Let's go home."

I tried to say something to him. To let him know I

didn't want to jump. But my jaw only opened and closed wordlessly.

Suddenly, I was facing the cliff again.

My left foot rose and planted itself so close to the drop-off that my toes actually extended out over the edge. A second later, my right foot followed suit.

I watched as pebbles and dirt skittered into the chasm and plummeted out of sight. My pulse roared in my ears. I tried to order my feet to take me back to safe ground, but they wouldn't obey.

Instead, I leapt forward. But I didn't fall. I floated. And my body buzzed with bliss.

I hovered, admiring the spectacular scenery from high above, perfectly safe and secure. A vivid blue river snaked happily through a lush green pasture dotted with wild flowers of every hue. Even from this height, I could make out the colorful butterflies that fluttered lazily from blossom to blossom. I had never seen anything so beautiful.

"Come on, guys!" I shouted to my friends. "It's amazing! Join me!"

With a grin, Sam stepped forward. "Sure, Sven. Great idea!"

He leapt off the edge, and I watched in horror as he instantly fell away toward the ground, screaming.

The scream abruptly ended.

Alicia loped forward. "Wait for me, Sam! Here I come!"

I tried to tell her to stop. But all that came out of my mouth was an uncontrollable giggle. In a heartbeat, she was gone, plunging to the broken granite shards below with a terrified screech.

My throat constricted with shock. Before I could even think of making a sound, Will, laughing, took a swan dive off the cliff. "This is awesome, Sven! Wheeeee!" His laugh turned into a shriek before cutting off altogether.

And then I was completely alone. They were gone. And it was my fault. I'd killed them.

A thin, cold voice called to me from nowhere. *Why the long face, Sven? This is exactly what you want, isn't it?*

Despite the horror of watching my only friends fall to their deaths, I felt the corners of my mouth twitch up into a smile.

My eyes snapped open. Pale morning sunlight filtered in through the RV's grimy windows.

My breath came in short, shallow gasps, and my mouth felt like someone had crammed it full of dandelion fluff. Pins and needles prickled up and down my left arm.

I let out a strangled squawk. And something on my left stirred. Sometime during the night, Ivy had wormed her way under my arm and wedged herself there. A thin trickle of drool threaded out of the corner of her mouth, leaving a wet patch on my shirt.

The RV's tires droned against the road beneath us. We were moving.

"Where are we?" I asked.

Sam glanced at me in the rearview mirror. "Ah, you're awake. Good. We're nearly there."

Outside, rugged brown prairie stretched out as far

as I could see, dotted here and there with stunted shrubs and the occasional gnarled tree.

"Where's there?"

"Cody, Wyoming, man," 808 announced. "Home of Four Omicron."

My mind buzzed with anxious thoughts of what we were about to face, until I distracted myself by counting the modest one-story houses that began appearing on either side of the road. Soon, we entered Cody. I watched a procession of motels, fast-food joints, gas stations, and car dealerships flash by.

"Here we are, folks," 808 called out as we pulled into a small parking lot. "You have reached your destination."

I looked out through the dust-caked window. A one-story house with crooked green shutters squatted at the edge of the lot. A sign perched atop two wooden stakes stood by the front door, its letters barely legible against a background of peeling white paint.

CODY ANIMAL HEALTH CENTER

ARNOLD SCHLUMPF, DVM

"So what do we do now?" Dix asked.

Alicia slung her backpack over her shoulder and opened the door of the RV. "Let's go find a dog."

We followed her out to the parking lot. Before we got halfway across the small expanse of cracked asphalt, the clinic door opened and a pleasant-looking middle-aged man dressed in black pants and a white lab coat stepped out.

"Hi there. Welcome to the Cody Animal Health Center! I'm Doctor Arnold Schlumpf." The man waved at us and flashed a warm smile. "How may I help you? We have a special on liver fluke preventative this month."

"Tempting," Alicia said. "But I think we'd rather talk to you about the dog."

Dr. Schlumpf scratched his head. "Ah, you're looking to adopt a dog. Wonderful. We have plenty to choose from. They all need good homes."

"Is that Four Omicron's overseer?" I whispered to 808, who had hitched a ride on my shoulder.

"Yup. That's him."

I shook my head. "Is he a weird flesh sac stuffed with gross things or is he normal?"

"Hey!" 808 objected. "What's that supposed to mean?"

"What's *what* supposed to mean?"

"'*Normal,*'" the scorpipede hissed. "Are you suggesting I'm somehow *abnormal* just because I lived inside a humanoid meat pouch with eight hundred seven other Synthetic bugs? Maybe you're the one who's not normal! Ever think of that?"

"Actually, yes," I told him. "Now be quiet."

Alicia stared the vet down. "We don't want to adopt a dog. We're looking for Four Omicron."

"Four Omicron?" Dr. Schlumpf furrowed his brow. "Four Omicron . . . oh, you must mean *Thor.* Four Omicron is a terrible name for a dog. I prefer to call him Thor. Let me get him for you."

Dr. Schlumpf whistled, and a dog who looked exactly like the one I had seen in the forest watering hole came trotting out of the clinic. He sat obediently on the pavement.

"Why is he making this so easy?" I asked 808.

The little scorpipede just shrugged his many shoulders. "Maybe he's cool like us, you know? Not on board with the whole killing-all-humans gig."

I hoped that was true. But the knot in my stomach gave me the feeling it wasn't.

Dr. Schlumpf grinned at us. "Thor here is a highly intelligent animal. He knows some wonderful tricks. Let me show you. Thor, down."

The dog immediately lay down.

"Thor, sit."

The dog sat.

"Thor, shake hands."

The dog extended a paw.

"You see? He's very well trained. Oh, but I almost forgot my favorite," the vet continued. "Watch this! Thor . . . *destroy your enemies!*"

CHAPTER 24.0:

\ < value= [New Dog, Old Trick] \ >

THE DOG LOOKED UP AT DR. SCHLUMPF and cocked his head questioningly.

The veterinarian's smile disappeared, instantly replaced by an angry scowl. "Don't just sit there, you mutt! Destroy your enemies! Now!" He punctuated his order with a swift kick to the dog's ribs.

Thor yelped.

"Come on, dummy!" Dr. Schlumpf snarled. "Destroy them! Do as I say!" He smacked the dog's head with his hand.

Thor shrank from the man. He looked up fearfully, then let out a single, loud bark.

A rustling began in the woods surrounding the parking lot. Twigs snapped. Leaves shook. It was like the forest around us had suddenly come to life.

Then we saw why.

Wild animals flooded into the parking lot from every direction. Some were big, and some were small. But all were angry. Wolves, squirrels, bison, mountain lions, hawks, bats, snakes, grizzly bears. They all gathered around Thor, as if looking to the dog for instructions.

"Very good." Dr. Schlumpf grinned. "Now kill the humans and these Synthetic traitors!"

A moment passed. Thor's hesitation earned him a kick. He yelped, then let out another bark.

Every animal in the parking lot turned to face us.

We didn't wait to see what they'd do next. We all scrambled as quickly as we could back into the RV. Outside, the animals surrounded us. Sam fumbled with the keys. Before he could insert them into the ignition, a bison slammed into the side of the motor home. The jolt sent the keys skittering across the floor.

The window next to me shattered as the huge antler

of a moose punched through it. Cubes of tempered glass rained down on me like hailstones.

And then the birds came. Dozens of them. Songbirds, woodpeckers, falcons. A bald eagle perched on the edge of the window frame and snapped its razor-edged beak at my face. It clicked shut an inch from my eye with a sharp *CLACK*. I fell backward onto the floor.

"Whoa!" cried 808, who was still clinging to my shoulder. "You could squash a guy throwing your body around like that!"

"Well, maybe you should have warned us that Four Omicron could do this!" I countered.

"In fairness, you never asked," the scorpipede replied.

I sighed. "Fine. I'm asking now. What is the dog programmed to do?"

"Pretty obvious, isn't it?" 808 said. "He's programmed to raise a massive animal army and use it to exterminate the humans. That's why he's here. Cody, Wyoming, has the biggest concentration of dangerous animals in the country. It's the perfect place. Pretty clever, really."

A tiny sparrow swooped down and nearly snatched 808 from my shoulder with its talons.

"Hey, watch it," he yelled, shaking a handful of tiny fists at the bird. "I ain't no bird food!"

I looked around the motor home. My friends were flailing their arms, frantically trying to fend off the birds. Some large creature was bashing at the side door. If it got in, we were finished.

As I watched a trio of yellow-and-black birds circle overhead, time seemed to slow to a crawl. The deafening flutter of wings faded away into silence. And it was replaced with the voice. That cold, alien voice in my head.

Let them die, Sven. It's what you want. It's all for the best.

I felt my muscles relax. The adrenaline that had been coursing through my system dissipated, leaving me tired and weak. I felt like I was sinking comfortably into the floor of the motor home.

Just let it happen.

I lay back and watched the scene unfold as if it were

being projected on a screen in front of me. Vivid, but entirely unreal.

Until something heavy landed on me. It was Will. And suddenly I was back in Sam's RV, listening as the squawks of the birds mingled with the screams of my friends.

Will rolled off me and flattened himself on the floor. It took every scrap of strength I had, but I forced myself to my feet and lurched toward the shattered window. I spotted Thor sitting on the gravel barking and yipping commands. If I wanted to save my friends, I had to stop him. "Thor!" I called. "Hey, Thor!"

The dog's ears twitched toward the sound of my voice. He looked at me from across the parking lot and cocked his head.

"Hey, boy!" I continued in a friendly voice. "You're a good dog! Why don't you call off the animals? Who's a good dog?"

Thor fixed me with his liquid brown eyes. And for a second, the birds paused, hovering in place.

Then Dr. Schlumpf whistled sharply and the dog turned away from me to continue the attack.

I had to get to him. I had to stop this assault.

I pushed my way toward the door, squeezing by Sam and Dix, who now stood back-to-back, trying to beat away the dive-bombing birds. As I passed the little dining table, my eyes fell on the remnants of Ivy's barbecue lunch from the day before. I snatched up one of the rib bones and jostled the last few feet to the RV's door.

Ivy appeared in front of me. "Where are you going?"

"I have to stop him," I explained.

She looked up me, her eyes gleaming. "Those animals will get you!"

"And if I stay here, the animals will get us all. I have to try."

"No!" Ivy insisted. "I only just got a big brother! I can't lose him now!"

"Ivy," I pleaded. "I can't just sit here."

She searched my face. Her lip quivered. Finally, she stepped out of my way.

Despite the warmth of the morning, the doorknob felt freezing. I hesitated as something thumped heavily against it from outside. I took a deep breath and pushed the door open.

"Hey there, Thor!" I called in the kindest voice I could. "That's a good boy. You're just a cuddly little puppy, aren't you?"

Thor's head swiveled toward me. A half dozen snarling coyotes grew silent and stepped back.

I cautiously lowered my foot to the ground. "I have something for you, boy! A nice treat." I held the rib bone up where he could see it.

His pink tongue poked out and ran a circuit around his mouth. A bison with long horns stepped to the side, clearing the way for me to approach Thor.

"Good boy!" I continued.

More animals parted in front of me. I stepped forward gingerly, keeping my movements slow and deliberate.

I ventured a glance back at the motor home. The birds had suspended their assault for the time being, and the vehicle's five occupants peered out at me. Will drummed his fingers against the windowsill. Dixon's jaw muscles flexed as he anxiously clenched his teeth. Ivy stared at me, her eyes bulging behind the lenses of her glasses. Sam muttered something over and over again. Alicia gave me a brisk nod.

I continued my slow march to Thor. When I finally reached him, I squatted down and held my face level with his. A low growl rattled through his body. I could feel the surrounding animals tense.

"It's okay, boy. I'm a friend," I said gently. "Here."

I offered him the rib bone. Thor opened his mouth and carefully took the bone between his teeth. I gradually curled my fingers behind his ear and gave him a scratch.

"What the heck are you doing, you stupid mutt?" Dr. Schlumpf thundered, kicking at Thor. "This is your enemy. Kill him!"

"It's okay, boy. I really am your friend. I promise. I'm not like that mean Dr. Schlumpf."

Dr. Schlumpf grabbed Thor by the back of the neck and shook him roughly. "Do what you've been trained to do! Destroy your enemies! Now!"

The dog's brown eyes turned up to mine for just a

moment. Then he barked. The animals that had paused their attack launched into motion. Something knocked me to the ground.

I looked up to see a grizzly bear rear up on its hind legs and let out a deafening roar.

CHAPTER 25.0:

\ < value= [A Full Moon Rising] \ >

THE BEAR RAISED ONE OF ITS IMMENSE arms. I couldn't tear my eyes from the deadly three-inch claws that jutted from its huge paws. I froze, waiting for the end to come. The bear swung its arm.

And Dr. Schlumpf flew halfway across the parking lot.

"Hey!" the Tick veterinarian screamed. "Not me! You're supposed to kill your enemies!"

For a moment, every animal stood motionless. Thor let out one last bark. As one, an army of snarling creatures descended on Dr. Schlumpf. When they dispersed back into the woods half a minute later, all that was left of him was a tattered white lab coat.

Something wet and warm slapped against my face. It was Thor's tongue. The dog yipped happily.

"I knew you were a good boy, Thor!" I told him. "Now that that big mean Dr. Schlumpf is gone, you're just a sweet little pooch, aren't you?"

I got to my feet and walked back to the RV. Thor followed on my heels, proudly carrying the bone I had given him.

"Seriously, Sven?" Alicia huffed. "Are you *trying* to get yourself killed?"

"What? It worked, didn't it? I don't see why you're so bent out of shape."

She gave me a hard, unblinking stare. After a few seconds, she looked away. "Whatever."

"Big bro!" Ivy scampered down the motor home's steps and threw her arms around my waist. "I'm so glad you're okay! How did you know he wasn't going to have the animals attack you?"

I shrugged. "I didn't. But after seeing how awful Dr. Schlumpf was to him, I figured maybe he just needed a little kindness."

"That was pretty awesome, dude!" Will told me.

Dix hopped down and put his arm around me. "Nice job, Sven! That was really smart thinking! And bonus—now we have a pet!"

"Hope you're not too disappointed it's not a monkey," I replied with a smirk.

Dix's smile faded. "Uh, yeah. I guess I made a pretty lousy first impression on you guys with that monkey thing, huh? I can't believe that was, like, the most important thing in the world to me."

"You mean it's not anymore?" Will asked.

Dix raised his eyebrows. "Well . . . maybe number two."

"So what now?" Alicia shifted her weight from foot to foot impatiently. "By my count, there are still three Ticks out there. Where do we find them?"

I grinned at her. "I think I can help with that. 808, my friend: Where to next?"

"Beats me," 808 said.

My grin disappeared. "What? I thought you were connected to the Tick network. I mean, you brought us here."

"Yeah, about that." 808 hesitated. "It looks like I've been locked out of the network. Guess they realized I was helping you guys out."

Alicia dabbed at a bloody scratch on her cheek with a tissue she had pulled out of her backpack. "So we're at a dead end?"

We all looked at one another.

It was Dix who broke the silence. "Maybe not. Ivy, Sven, and I are all Ticks, right? Sven and I were adopted, and Ivy was in foster care. Because we weren't born to human parents. We were . . ." He swallowed hard and spat the words out. "We were *made*. And then we were placed among humans to help us blend in. You with me so far?"

"Tell us something we don't know, brainiac," Ivy said.

"I'm getting to that," Dix told her. "So I was thinking there must be some sort of records for adoptions. There has to be a lot of paperwork to fill out and stuff. If we can see the records, maybe we can find them that way. Sven said the next two Ticks are twins. All we have to do is find twins that were adopted over the last, let's say, fifteen years . . ." He left the rest of his argument unsaid.

The hint of a frown played across Alicia's face. "That doesn't seem like the type of information they'd just post on the Internet for anyone to see. And besides, there must be millions of adoption records out there. Even if we could access them, it'd take weeks to go through them all."

"Yeah, you're probably right," he responded. "So let's hear your better idea."

Alicia scratched an abstract pattern in the gravel with her toe.

The public library in Cody was a modern, angular building situated next to a placid little pond. We walked through the lobby and made our way to the computer room, where a dozen desktop machines sat atop a double row of tables that lined the moss-green walls.

"Take a computer," Sam instructed. "If you find an online database of adoption records, let everyone know, and we'll help search it."

The six of us each sat and started our searches. Thor lay down, curled up on my feet, and closed his eyes. Within seconds, he was snoring.

It didn't take long for me to realize how hopeless the whole exercise was. Each state had its own rules and regulations regarding what type of information was available, and most had a whole series of hoops you had to jump through just to even *start* looking at records. It was like looking for a needle in fifty different haystacks, each of which was protected by a ten-foot-tall electric fence.

Still, we had to try. I clicked on one link after another, but each led to a dead end. Then, one led to a different kind of end.

"Hey!" I cried as the screen of my computer suddenly filled with the image of . . . something. It was fleshy and sort of roundish with streaks of black scrawled on its surface.

"What the heck?" Alicia blurted. "What *is* that?"

"Is it a piece of fruit?" Dixon asked. The computer in front of him displayed the same photo.

Will's monitor showed the image too. "No, I think it's a—"

"It's a butt!" Ivy yowled.

"Is *that* what it is?" 808 asked. "Huh. There was one

of those on the Bing flesh sac, but I only ever saw it from the inside."

It *was* a butt. A butt with the words *HA! HA!* written on it in black ink.

I looked around the room. Every monitor in the place showed the same image!

"What's going on?" Dix wondered. "Why is there a big old heinie on our screens?"

"Because someone's mooning us," Ivy explained. "Duh!"

Thor, who had been woken up by all the commotion, yawned and looked at me, blinking sleepily. He glanced at my monitor and growled at the derriere.

I navigated to a different website, but the butt was still there. I tried three or four more URLs—nothing changed.

"It's like the whole Internet is just one big keister!" Will remarked. "I mean, it'd be kinda funny if we didn't have the world to save."

Alicia pulled out her phone. "Maybe it's just the computers here. Let me see if . . . nope, it's on my phone, too."

"It looks like someone's hacked the Internet," Sam said, scratching his bird's nest of grizzled hair. "The *entire* Internet."

"Is that even possible?" I asked. "I know there have been some serious cyberattacks against individual sites. Even groups of sites. But the whole Web?"

"Apparently." Sam's expression was grim. "And without the Internet, we may be dead in the water."

CHAPTER 26.0:

\ < value= [Nothing Butt Problems] \ >

THE FUR ALONG THOR'S BACK ROSE INTO stiff spikes, and he growled angrily at my computer monitor.

"What is it, boy? What's wrong?" I asked.

Needless to say, he didn't answer. But he did place his front legs on the table and paw at the monitor.

"He doesn't like the tushy," Alicia said. "I can't blame him."

I had been trying to avoid looking at the butt any more than absolutely necessary. But the way Thor was acting . . . it was like he was trying to call our attention to something on that screen. So I gritted my teeth and looked the butt right in the face.

It was pretty much like any other rump. Except, of course, for the words. Maybe what Thor was reacting to wasn't the butt. Maybe there was something else in the photo that bothered him.

In the upper-right corner of the image, a patch of blue sky speckled with fluffy white clouds was visible through a window in the background.

I leaned in close and squinted at that corner. It was pretty overexposed, but I could just make out something in the sky.

A dark shape. Something blackish and roundish and—

I gasped, sucking a sharp breath in through my teeth as I recognized the shape of that object.

"Guys! Look at this!" I pointed at the screen. "There's . . . there's a UFO in this picture!"

Will grabbed my shoulder and squeezed hard. "Oh my gosh! The Ticks are in this with the aliens! It's worse than we thought!"

Alicia leaned over to look at my screen. "Please. It's *not* a UFO." She grabbed my mouse and zoomed in on the dark shape. As the image grew to fill the screen, more details emerged. Soon we could see the flying saucer wasn't a flying saucer at all.

"See? It's a building." She pointed at the towering supports that held up the flying saucer–shaped top of the structure. "It looks familiar to me."

"It's the Space Needle. In Seattle," Dix informed us.

"Yeah, right." Ivy rolled her eyes. "*Space Needle*. You're totally making that up."

"That's what it's called. It's a big landmark in Seattle," he explained patiently. "I played there just a couple of weeks ago for a three-night run. Roz wouldn't let me out of the hotel room, so all I could do was sit there and look out the window. And *that's* what I was looking at."

"Okay, well, that explains the UFO. But then what's *that*?" Will pressed his finger against the screen.

There was definitely something there. It was flesh-colored and shaped a little like a slipper.

"An ear, reflected in the window!" I said as my brain finally made sense of the cluster of pixels Will was pointing at. "It must be the ear that's attached to the person attached to that booty!"

"I think it's safe to assume that whoever is in this picture is behind the hack," Sam reasoned.

Dix looked at him. "Do you think taking down the Internet might be part of the Ticks' plan?"

Sam shrugged. "All I know for sure is whoever did this possesses a level of sophistication that's beyond anything I've seen before."

I blurted, "They're mooning the entire Internet! That doesn't seem so sophisticated to me!"

"All I mean," Sam explained, "is that it's long been believed that this kind of Internet-wide outage was impossible. Hackers might be able to target individual companies or even regions, but taking down the entire Web? Anyone who can do that is doing some next-level stuff."

"What are we going to do?" Will shifted his weight from one foot to another. "I know searching adoption records was a long shot. But without being able to get online, it's no shot at all."

"I think we should try to find out more about this

picture," Alicia suggested. "Let me pull up the source code. I heard sometimes hackers leave kind of a clue or something. Like they're daring people to find them."

She right-clicked on the butt and selected *View Page Source* from the menu that appeared.

A new window appeared on the monitor.

```
1  <!DOCTYPE html [
2  <!ENTITY % htmlDTD
3  PUBLIC "-//W3C//DTD XHTML 1.0 Strict//EN"
4  "DTD/xhtml1-strict.dtd">
5  %htmlDTD:
6  <!ENTITY % "there once was a butt like a
   STar">
7  <!ENTITY % "whose owner was bound to
   go far">
8  <!ENTITY % "ALOHA. he said">
9  <!ENTITY % "you'll all soon be dead">
10 <!ENTITY % "in the WEST I am called
   chapeau noir">
11 Sayonara. losers!
```

"What's *that*?" Dix asked pointing at the only words we could make out among the jumble of characters.

After processing the lines for half a dozen seconds, I knew what we were looking at. "It's a limerick."

"A what-rick?" Ivy asked.

"A limerick. It's a silly form of poetry. My dad used to try to make them up at the dinner table. He thought they were hilarious. They weren't."

Sam copied the words on a scrap of paper and read it aloud a couple of times. "Hmmm. *Chapeau noir.* French for 'black hat.' It's a term that hackers use to describe bad guys."

"Yeah, well, all I see is a bad piece of poetry," 808 said. "Whoever wrote that deserves a good stinging!"

"Forget the limerick." Alicia closed the source code. "I want to know more about that reflection. I wish we could see the face that goes with that ear."

Will cleared his throat. "Maybe we can. Sam, do you have any photo editing software on your laptop?"

In Sam's RV a few minutes later, Will fired up the laptop, saved a copy of the butt picture, and opened it in an application called PhotoEditER.

"I went to computer camp last summer," Will narrated as he clicked through various settings and filters. "We did this whole unit on digital design. There are all kinds of things you can do to bring out different colors and details in images."

He dragged a bunch of sliders left and right. The picture went blue and then red and then bright and then dark. Eventually, Will's mouse-clicking slowed and finally stopped.

"Check this out!" Will declared. "I messed with the contrast and the brightness. And I bumped up the highlights and . . . well, look! We have a face! Right there in the window!"

My stomach did a flip. I knew the grinning face reflected in that window! I had seen it before when I was inside the deer's head. It belonged to a Tick. An Omicron like me.

"You know what this means?" I asked.

Will scratched his nose. "What?"

I stood up. "We just found the butt that needs kicking."

CHAPTER 27.0:

\ < value= [Thumbs-up!] \ >

"SO LET ME GET THIS STRAIGHT." SAM looked at me with more than a flicker of doubt. "You think the boy you saw in the deer's mind is the same one whose face was reflected in a window somewhere in Seattle."

"I *know* it was him," I corrected.

"So let's say for the sake of argument it's him—"

"It is!" I interrupted. The expressionless faces of those Ticks in that pond were indelibly imprinted on my memory.

"Fine. I *believe* you," he said, even though his expression made it clear he wasn't sure. "But how are we going to find him?"

I scratched my head. "Maybe we can figure it out. We could see the Space Needle through the window, right? How many places in Seattle would have a view like that?"

"Um, all of them?" Dix answered. "The Space Needle is, like, *the* landmark for the whole city. And with all the hills in Seattle, you can see it from everywhere."

My heart sank a little. How on earth were we going to find the mooning boy and his twin sister? All we had was a city.

Alicia stood up. "Well, we can't just sit here and wait for the end of the world!" she declared. "We have to go to Seattle! Come on, Sam! Drive!"

Sam just slumped lower in his seat and gave a half-hearted shrug. "Mmnnnggghhh," he muttered.

Alicia turned to Dixon. "You're with me, right?"

Dix looked at his shoes.

"Will?" She locked her eyes on him. Her eyebrows arched in a wordless plea.

"Ummm . . ." That's all Will managed to get out before he started compulsively opening and closing a cupboard door.

She regarded each of us in turn. No one met her gaze. Even Thor refused to swivel his eyes in her direction.

Her eyes landed on me. I tried to smile but produced something more like a grimace. "Um . . . well, I guess . . ." I wanted to humor her, but the sheer impossibility of tracking down a single Tick in a city packed with hundreds of thousands of people tied my tongue in a tangle of knots.

"Fine!" Alicia raged. "I'll get there myself! I'll find those Ticks! And I'll stop them even if I have to hitchhike."

Without another word, she opened the door and stormed out. We all watched as she stalked across the parking lot and stopped by the side of the road. Even though there wasn't a single car in sight, she raised her thumb and held it out toward the empty stretch of asphalt.

I tried to beat back the achy sensation building somewhere behind my sternum. We'd been through so much together over the past several days that I felt almost as close to her as I did to Will. She could have killed me when she first discovered I was a Tick. But she hadn't. More than that, she'd risked *her* life to save mine. And she'd barely escaped alive.

My face burned with shame. I couldn't bail on her now. She'd lost her parents to the Ticks. She'd left the Settlement in Chernobyl—all by herself—to try to put a stop to the Ticks' plans.

Finding a couple of Ticks hidden in a big city may be impossible. But if Alicia was willing to attempt the impossible, I sure as heck wasn't going to leave her to do it alone.

I stood up, left the motor home, and joined her by the side of the road. I didn't say a word. I just stuck my arm out and raised my thumb.

She turned her head in my direction and gave me a curt nod before swiveling her gaze back to the empty stretch of pavement.

A few minutes later, another thumb joined ours.

Will!

I slung my arm around his shoulder.

"Got room for one more?" Dixon asked, adding his thumb to the collection.

"*Two* more, you mean, dummy," Ivy corrected, lifting her tiny thumb toward the sky.

We watched as a small object a mile or two down the street resolved itself into a car. But it made a left turn onto a dirt road a few hundred yards before it reached us and disappeared from sight.

Something wet glided across the back of my hand. It was Thor's tongue. He planted his butt down in the dirt and sat patiently with us, panting in the hot midday sun.

And there we stood. Six chumps on an absurd quest. Waiting for a free ride to failure.

Until a seventh thumb joined in—a short, stubby thumb that was kind of hairy.

"Um, Sam?"

"Yes, Sven?" He stared straight ahead at a rusty road sign that trembled slightly in the gentle breeze.

"Why are you here?"

"It was kind of lonely in the RV all by myself," he told me. "Anyway, if you're ready, maybe we should get going. It's a long drive to Seattle."

Sam, his gut straining at the fabric of his top, swung himself into the driver's seat. The ancient engine let out a long, asthmatic wheeze before coughing to life.

As we rolled through the streets of Cody, Ivy gave me a questioning stare. "I don't get it. How can a picture of this kid's stupid butt all over the Internet help destroy humanity? That's what he's supposed to do, right?"

I pointed out the window. "Look. It hasn't even been two hours yet."

We passed a bank that had a large sign taped to the front door. SORRY, NO WITHDRAWALS.

That hadn't stopped a large crowd from gathering in front of the building, rattling the locked doors and screaming.

"It's my money!" a woman dressed in a sharp business suit screamed.

A man clad in grimy overalls tried to push in front of her. A second later, he was on his back end, holding his hand up to a heavily bleeding nose.

The woman stood above him, shaking her fist and glowering. "Try to cut in front of me again and I'll kill you!"

We passed a line of cars a mile long, motionless along the side of the road like a humungous dead metallic snake. The giant queue of vehicles ended at a gas station. A large piece of weathered plywood was propped up in front of the pumps. NO GAS, it read in neon orange letters.

I turned to Ivy. "It's not just his butt on the Internet. I have a feeling he's hacking into *everything*. Stores, banks, gas stations."

"And when he takes down critical infrastructure, like electric grids and water pumping stations . . . ," Alicia began.

". . . we're all doomed," I finished.

CHAPTER 28.0:
\ < value= [I Get Some Air] \ >

NOW WOULD BE THE PERFECT TIME, SVEN. *While they're sleeping. Finish them all. It's what you want. You're a Tick. The humans don't care about you. They hate you. And you hate them, don't you, Sven? So, what are you waiting for? Kill them now.*

My eyes snapped open. I leapt up from the couch where I had been sleeping. The cold, distant voice was in my head again. Only now it seemed a lot less distant.

I looked around the RV. Alicia was sleeping with her head on the dining table. Will was curled into a ball on the bench across from her. Ivy muttered, lost in a dream, leaning against Dix, who snoozed next to her on the couch. Even Thor was asleep, his legs twitching as he dreamed about whatever it was Synthetic dogs dreamed about. Electric sheep, maybe? A snore as loud as a chain saw came from the driver's seat, where Sam was slumped over the steering wheel.

I pressed my hot forehead against the cool glass of the window and looked outside. We had stopped in a campground parking lot alongside a few other RVs and trailers that shone in the cold pale blue light of the full moon overhead. A sign at the edge of the parking lot read, CRYSTAL GLACIER NATIONAL PARK, LITTLE FALLS, MONTANA.

As the last echoes of the voice died away, I realized my hands were balled into fists. I took a deep breath.

And for one brief moment, something deep inside me told me the voice was right. I mean, it made sense. I wasn't actually human. So why would I expect any human to care about me? When it really came down to it, could I ever be accepted by them? Even my friends might not stand by me if they had to choose between me and a real kid. Maybe I should just do what the voice said. . . .

No! I'd never hurt my friends!

I burst through the RV's door and out into the crisp, clear night. Countless stars glittered overhead in the Montana sky—more than I'd ever seen before in my life.

When I heard that voice, it felt like some *other* was inside my head. Like a finger poking through the shell of a hard-boiled egg. But it also felt just a tiny bit . . . natural. Like it was a part of me.

How could those feelings coexist? It was like there was a war in my head between the programming that made me "human" and the hardware that came standard with every Synthetic.

I didn't think I would ever actually hurt my friends. Then again, a week ago I never would have imagined I was a Synthetic programmed to wipe out the human race. What if one day I listened to the voice and did something horrible to them? What if it got to the point where I was no longer me, but just an empty husk, controlled by the voice? It had been getting steadily louder and more insistent. Would it keep growing? And if it did, would I always be able to stop myself from doing what it wanted?

Maybe it would be best if I disappeared for a while.

I could take off now and let the others save the world without me. It's not like I was that useful to them anyway. I was just some weird kid who ate gross things.

Suddenly, I knew what I needed to do.

I looked toward the thick, towering bank of pine trees that marked the limit of the camping area. Despite the bright moon, those woods seemed to swallow up any light completely. They could swallow me up as well. I took a step toward the shadows, but a hand on my shoulder stopped me.

"Where are you going?" Alicia asked.

"I . . . uh, erm, I . . ." I choked on my words.

Alicia sat on the bench and patted the space next to her.

"What's going on with you, Sven? You've been acting . . . a little funny lately."

I managed a weak smile. "A little funny? I'm the robot kid that eats stuff."

"That's not what I mean," she replied, fixing me with a green stare. "You've been . . . just . . . not yourself."

I wanted to tell her about the voice. But I hesitated. What would she think? What would she *do*?

"You can tell me if something's going on, you know," she said gently, when the silence got kind of awkward.

"I . . . hear this voice. In my head. It started when we were traveling to New York City, and it's spoken to me a few times since. And it's getting louder."

"What does it say?"

"It . . . it tells me you and Will and the others aren't really my friends." I paused to rub my eyes with my fingertips. "And it says I should . . . well . . . kill you."

"Do you think someone's trying to hack into you?" she asked. "Like Dr. Shallix did before. Maybe that kid in Seattle is doing it."

I shrugged. "I worry it's . . . even worse than that."

"What do you mean?"

"I mean," I said, taking a deep breath to try to steady my voice. "What if it's not coming from the outside?"

"I don't get what you're saying. If *what's* not coming from outside?"

"The voice. I mean, what if it's not someone trying to hack me? What if it's my programming? What if I really do want to kill you?"

CHAPTER 29.0:

\ < value= [We Decide to Get Takeout] \ >

ALICIA GASPED. "SVEN, NO! THAT'S NOT you! You know that."

"Really? Until last week, I thought I was just like any other human. But I'm really just some kind of machine that's putting you and everyone else in danger."

A laugh snorted out of her. "*You're* putting us in danger? Sven, you saved us from Thor and those animals, like, twelve hours ago. And you saved Will and me from killing each other when Dix was singing. Not to mention Dr. Shallix. As I recall, you were the one who stopped him. We'd be dead three or four times over if it hadn't been for you. So would the entire human race, probably."

"Well, yeah, but—"

She cut me off. "Shut up about putting us in danger and get back in the motor home before I kick your butt all the way to Seattle."

The first 257 miles of the drive to Seattle were uneventful. The 258th, however, was when things started to go wrong. The RV coughed and spluttered before going eerily silent. We coasted to a stop at the side of the road.

"Are we there yet?" Ivy asked, leaping out of her seat.

"The answer is still no," Sam told her. "We're out of gas."

"Well, why didn't you stop at a gas station?" she asked, her eyebrows furrowed accusingly behind her glasses.

"The gas stations were out of commission, remember?" Dixon replied. "Whatever this hacker's doing, he wants to make sure nobody has any gas."

Alicia rapped her knuckles on the laminate tabletop. "Sam, where are we?"

Sam squinted at the map. "I think we're only a few miles east of Waterton, Idaho. So, we're not far from civilization. The bad news—being a few miles east of Waterton, Idaho, means we're still . . ." He measured out the distance with his thumb. ". . . more than three hundred miles from Seattle."

"Ugh!" Will moaned. "That's a long way to walk."

Alicia snatched up her backpack. "Forget that! I'm getting a lift!"

She strode out of the RV and positioned herself by the side of the road, ready to flag down the next car.

The problem was, the only cars in sight were out of gas, left abandoned by the side of the road. It was like something out of a zombie movie. Even here, on one of the biggest interstate highways in the country, there was nothing but dead cars everywhere. And Sam's RV was now one of them.

I walked out after Alicia. "I think you're going to be waiting awhile. Businesses are closed. Gas stations aren't pumping. Nobody's on the road."

Alicia kicked at the ground, scattering gravel across the pavement. "Then we walk!"

"We can't walk that—"

She shut me up with a glare that could have melted

glass. "I'm not giving up! I didn't lose everything just to roll over and play dead! Don't you understand that? I'm stopping the Ticks. If it takes me a week to walk to Seattle, fine. If it takes me a month, it takes me a month. But I'm not giving up!"

I think she realized as well as I did that a week would be too late. Whatever the next Tick in line was programmed to do, he was already doing it.

She turned to me. "You know this is just the beginning, right? I mean, look what's already happened in just half a day. They're going to take out electricity, communications, water, and food. I don't know about you, but I'd rather go out fighting."

I nodded grimly. "Me too. But how are we going to fight if we can't even get to Seattle?"

"I have a thought about that." Sam had walked up behind us with Ivy, Dix, Will, and Thor in tow. "The motor home has a diesel engine."

Ivy sighed. "So? There are no gas stations pumping gas. Your stupid motor home might as well run on diamonds. We can't get those, either."

"Not diamonds," Sam said. "Cooking oil."

Dix gave him a sidelong glance. "Like . . . oil you cook with?"

Sam nodded. "Exactly. Oil you cook with. When Rudolf Diesel invented the diesel engine, he actually used vegetable oil to run it. Peanut oil, if I recall correctly. The engine's design hasn't changed that much over the years. Plenty of people have converted their diesel engines to run on cooking oil. We can too."

"Great!" Ivy cried in mock excitement, following it up with a mock pout. "Oh wait, I left my hundred-gallon tub of peanut oil at home. Darn!"

Will cleared his throat and pointed to a blue-and-white sign a hundred yards ahead of us on the side of the road.

FOOD · GAS · LODGING

NEXT EXIT

"Look. Food," he said. "Restaurants cook food. And to cook food they use—"

"Wait!" Ivy interrupted, holding her hand up to

silence Will. "I have an idea. We just need to get some cooking oil from a restaurant!"

Will blinked at her. "Hey, that was my . . . oh, never mind."

"One problem with Ivy's idea," Dixon pointed out. "We have to find a restaurant that's open and will sell us some oil."

"Um, two problems, actually," Sam muttered. "Even if we do find an open restaurant, we're broke. I have no cash, and without the Internet, credit cards aren't working."

Ivy grinned. "I'll take care of it. Come on, Sven. Let's get some oil."

Without waiting for me to answer, she marched down the road in the direction of the exit.

"Go ahead, Sven," Sam said. "The rest of us will make the modifications to the fuel system. And if you can, get walnut oil. It has the lowest viscosity."

I nodded uncertainly and took off after Ivy. Thor trotted alongside me, his pink tongue dangling wetly from his mouth.

"Hot day, huh?" 808 remarked from my shoulder.

I wiped the sweat from my forehead and nodded.

The scorpipede continued, "So, uh, I don't suppose you'd mind if I look for a little, you know, shade. I'm frying here."

"Yeah, fine," I replied. "But where are you going to find . . ."

Before I could finish my question, he scuttled up my neck and nestled behind my ear.

"Ah, that's better," 808 sighed.

"Hey!" I objected loudly. "Haven't you ever heard of personal space?"

He laughed. "I lived in a man-shaped flesh sac with eight hundred seven other dudes my whole life. So the answer to your question is *no*. I'm gonna grab some shut-eye. Let me know if I miss anything."

The walk into town took about an hour. As soon as we arrived, I realized the sign announcing FOOD • GAS • LODGING had been using the terms very loosely. In fact, there was only one place to get food in the entire town. There was only one place to get gas. There was only one place to find lodging. And they all happened to be the same place.

VINNY'S CHINESE FOOD, GAS & LODGING proclaimed

an old, weatherworn sign that hung in front of a dilapidated two-story building.

On the steps leading up to the front door sat a grizzled-looking man in a pair of overalls and a tattered red flannel shirt. A scowl adorned the man's face; across his lap lay a large rifle. On either side of him were two pieces of cardboard bearing messages scrawled in thick black marker.

On one it said:

No Food

No Gas

No Lodging

On the other it said:

You Loot

I Shoot

Before Ivy, Thor, and I were within twenty feet of the man, who I assumed must have been Vinny himself, he called out, "That's far enough, pal. You better be on your way before someone gets hurt. And by '*someone*,' I mean you."

I raised my hands and spoke as calmly as I could.

"Uh, we're not looking for any trouble. Are you Vinny?"

The man scowled. "Who's askin'?"

"Just us," I told him mildly.

"What do you mean '*us*'?" Vinny replied. "Looks to me like you're all alone."

I looked around. Ivy and Thor were gone. They must have seen the gun and taken off. And I wasn't about to tell Vinny about the talking scorpipede sleeping behind my right ear.

I swallowed nervously and took a small step closer. "Oh, right. Well, it's okay. You see, we're . . . I mean *I'm* . . . just hoping to get some cooking oil. For our motor home. I mean *my* motor home. Do you have any?"

"Well, that depends," the man rumbled. "You got money?"

I shook my head.

Vinny laughed humorlessly. "You got no money, but you want to take *my* oil? In my book, that's stealing, pal. The folks I run with, we don't take too kindly to thieves. In fact, I'd say the only good thief . . . is a *dead* thief."

CHAPTER 30.0:

\ < value= [Oh, Rats!] \ >

I HAD A PROBLEM. IF I DIDN'T RETURN with oil, we'd never get to Seattle in time. But the only way to get oil was to get by an angry guy with a gun.

As the gears slowly turned in my head, I began to realize that not getting shot might be my best course of action.

I took a step back. "Sorry. You're right. I'll . . . I should just be going. . . ."

But then I froze. Directly behind the man, visible through the building's glass door, Ivy appeared, holding up a plastic jug and pointing to her wrist like she was wearing a watch. She'd snuck inside and found oil! And she needed more time!

I had to keep this guy from going inside and finding Ivy. As much as I hated the idea, I had to keep him focused on me.

"So," I said, tamping down my panic, "I've been meaning to ask. You must really like Chinese food, huh?" *Ugh! What a stupid question!*

"You know what I like? People who *don't* ask questions!" Vinny replied.

"Uh . . . sorry. So, if you don't have any oil you can give me, could you tell me where I might get some? Oops! That was a question, wasn't it? So was that. Sorry."

"What did I just say about questions, pal?" he snapped. "No. More. *Questions!*"

I wished I could take back my words. "Geez, why do you hate questions so much?" *Ugh! Another question! What the heck is wrong with me?*

He replied by standing up. "I'm gonna make this easy for you, kid. I'm gonna count to three. When I get to three, you're going to be gone, understand? And if you're not, you're gonna wish you were. One."

Uh-oh! I didn't know if my emergency repair system

could deal with being shot full of holes. But even if it could, the last thing I wanted was to find out.

"Two."

The seconds seemed to drag on for centuries, when, suddenly . . .

WOOF!

I looked up just in time to see Thor tear around the corner of the building. A seething carpet of black fuzz flowed across the ground behind him like an immense, hairy cape.

WOOF! Thor barked again and the black carpet changed direction and surged directly toward Vinny.

That's when I realized it wasn't a carpet at all, but *rats*! Thousands of rats! Thor must have summoned them from the row of battered garbage cans that lined the side of the building.

WOOF! A third bark, and the rats clambered all over the surly restaurant owner, wrenching the rifle out of his hands and dragging it out of reach. Vinny stumbled and fell flat on his back. The rats swarmed him, their tiny teeth biting into his clothing, holding him to the ground under the weight of thousands of little bodies.

"Ugh!" Vinny screamed. "I knew I should have hired an exterminator!"

Thor trotted over to me and licked my hand.

"Good boy!" I told him, scratching him behind the ear.

The restaurant's front door swung open. "Uh, Sven?" Ivy called. "If you're done playing with the dog, you could come in here and, you know, help me!"

I nodded and followed Ivy inside, carefully skirting Vinny and his blanket of rats.

Vinny's Chinese Food, Gas & Lodging wouldn't have been my first choice of restaurants. Actually, it wouldn't have been my ten thousandth choice of restaurants. The entire place smelled like the boys' bathroom at Chester A. Arthur Middle School—a combination of farts, sweat, and cleaning chemicals, mixed in with the delicate aroma of despair.

"Over here." Ivy gestured toward one of those doors inset with a little porthole that you see in pretty much every restaurant on the planet.

We pushed it open and walked into the kitchen,

which was the dirtiest place I had ever seen. And I've spent time in a Dumpster. Open buckets of used cooking oil littered the floor. Decades-old grease coated every surface, even hanging from the ceiling like stalactites.

Ivy dipped the jug she was carrying into a cold deep fryer filled with a gluggy, opaque liquid. "Come on, big bro," she said, nodding toward a stack of plastic takeout containers. "Start scooping."

I picked up a container and filled it. "How are we going to get all this oil back to the RV?"

"One step ahead of you, slowpoke." She grinned. "I already found a shopping cart behind the restaurant."

Halfway back to the RV, it dawned on me how much this plan sucked. Sure, it wasn't fun having Vinny point a gun at me. And it was pretty gross collecting all that used oil, which I could still feel trapped under my fingernails. But now, as Ivy and I lugged a rusty, three-wheeled shopping cart uphill, I knew the true meaning of the word *sucky*.

Sweat streamed out of every pore in my body, stinging my eyes and soaking my clothes. Flies, attracted by the rancid oil, swarmed around my face, scrabbling into my ears and nostrils, where, as far as I could tell, they were throwing little dance parties.

808 seemed to be enjoying himself, though. Every time a fly got too close, he'd snap it out of the air and devour it. "The flies out here are delicious," he remarked from behind my ear. "You should try one, Sven."

"No thanks," I muttered, trying futilely to wipe the sweat out of my eyes.

Something flitted by low overhead. Thor whimpered as its dark shadow slid over him. It circled us and let out a loud *caw-caw-caw-caw*, a cry that sounded more than a little like laughter. I shuddered as I finally figured out what it was. A watcher. A Tick designed for surveillance. I had seen crows just like the one wheeling above me now when I was back in Schenectady.

They'd been tracking us since we left Sam's place in Niagara Falls, I realized with dread. The Ticks had known exactly where we were and what we were doing the whole time!

The bird flew off, gleefully *caw-caw-cawing*, until it disappeared from sight.

Despite the blazing sun above me, my blood chilled in my veins.

CHAPTER 31.0:

\ < value= [A Rolling Deep Fryer] \ >

"WHAT TOOK YOU SO LONG?" ALICIA leaned against the side of the RV, gouging a trench in the gravel by the side of the road with the heel of her boot.

I glared at her. *"What?!"*

"Geez, take it easy, Sven," she grinned. "I was just busting your chops. Grow a sense of humor, why don't you?"

Will emerged from the RV and patted me on the back. "Eeew!" he cried, recoiling at the wet slap that rang out when his hand made contact with my sweat-soaked shirt. "You're sweaty."

"Well, as fun as lugging ninety-eight quarts of oil

for three miles uphill in a broken shopping cart might sound, it was kind of, you know, hard work."

"About that," 808 remarked, crawling out from behind my ear. "Didn't your mom ever tell you to wash behind your ears? Sheesh, it's not pretty back there!"

Sam slid out from under the RV and wiped his grimy hands on his pants. "Well, we've finished the modifications to the engine. So once we fill up with the oil, we should be ready to go."

"What did you do to the RV?" Ivy asked.

"It was pretty straightforward," Dixon answered, sticking his head out from the passenger's-side window. "We just had to take apart the thingy and run the other thing under the gas tank and along the stuff that goes into the thing in the engine."

Ivy and I stared at him. "What?" we said in unison.

Sam laughed. "While that's essentially right, maybe I can elucidate. As I mentioned, a diesel engine can run on cooking oil. The problem is, when it's cold, the oil is so thick and viscous it tends to gum up the engine. It's like . . . well, imagine trying to take a shower with rice pudding." He paused and licked his lips hungrily before continuing. "But if we keep the oil warm, it'll flow freely and won't clog up the fuel line or pump. All we had to do was take apart the RV's water heater, affix the electric heating elements to the outside of the gas tank and fuel line, and wire them up to the transformer. *Voilà!* The oil stays nice and warm, and we have a working engine."

I squinted at him. "But . . . but isn't attaching an electric heating element to a gas tank . . . I don't know . . . *dangerous*?"

He laughed. "Oh, please. It's perfectly safe." A dark cloud passed over his features. "Unless, of course, the gas tank ruptures."

"And what if it does?" Ivy asked, her eyes wide behind the lenses of her glasses.

"No time to waste, kids! Let's fill up the tank," Sam blurted.

Once we had emptied the takeout containers into the gas tank, we climbed inside and took our seats.

"All right, everyone, ready to give it a shot?" Sam

called from the driver's seat. "Dixon, my friend, hit the switch."

"Roger that, Sam." Dix stood up and flipped a switch on the wall near the bathroom. "Okay, it's on."

A low electrical hum met my ears.

After waiting about thirty seconds, Sam turned the key in the ignition. "Here it goes."

Rrraaaaawww rrarrarrraaaaww rrrraaawwwaawwaa . . .

The engine struggled to turn over. It sounded like a goat with a mouthful of peanut butter.

Rrrrrraaawwww rwwwaaaawwwrrrr . . .

RRRAOOOOOOAAAARRRRRR!!!

It actually started! I shook my head in amazement. I felt twenty pounds lighter from sheer relief.

We all cheered.

Right up until the smell hit.

"Ugh!" Will gagged. "What *is* that? It smells like . . . like *bad* Chinese food!"

"Bad Chinese food that's already been digested," Alicia said in a nasal voice, pinching her nostrils closed. "Where the heck did you get that oil, Sven? An outhouse?"

"Where did I get it? I walked miles to get it! And I nearly got shot in the process! Then I had to push every single drop of it back in a three-wheeled shopping cart! I can't believe you're complaining just because it smells a little!"

"Dude, it doesn't just smell *a little*. It smells like . . . like . . ." Will's voice dissolved into a series of gags.

"Sam, will this get better or are we going to have to deal with this the whole way to Seattle?" Alicia asked.

Whatever Sam's answer was, I didn't hear it. Because at that moment, the voice came back. It crowded out all other sounds; all other thoughts.

Listen to that. They hate you, Sven. The humans hate you for being a Synthetic. They hate you because you're not one of them. You can't trust them. You can only trust . . . your family. Your Synthetic brothers and sisters. You love them. And you hate the humans, Sven.

The voice was closer now. I got the feeling that the farther west we traveled, the louder and more real it would become. It echoed in my skull like the screech of a sneaker in an empty gymnasium. It wrapped itself around my brain, a steel net tightening and tightening until it became my whole world. It came from nowhere and everywhere at once. It shuddered through me, filling every molecule of my body with its irresistible logic. Over and over it spoke.

You hate them.

With each word, every muscle in my body tensed a little more, until my entire frame felt like a coiled spring, a hundred cobras ready to strike.

Stop the humans.

Do it now.

Stop them.

Stop them.

STOP THEM!

HURT THEM!

KILL THEM!

My heart raced. My hands tightened into fists. My teeth clenched. My eyelids pressed closed. I wanted to do exactly what the voice said. I wanted to hurt them. I wanted to . . . *kill* my friends.

CHAPTER 32.0:

\ < value= [Definitely Not the Voice of Reason] \ >

NO!

I battled against the words that invaded my consciousness.

"Shut up! Shut up! Shut up!" I screamed, leaping up and clamping my hands over my ears in a vain attempt to shut out the voice. "Get out of my head! Stop talking! Stop it! STOP!"

The voice spoke again.

Geez, dude! Relax. Fine, we'll deal with the smell. Just don't have a cow.

Wait. That . . . that wasn't the voice. It was . . . *Will*?

I opened my eyes.

Everyone was staring at me like I was a rabid gorilla that had escaped from the zoo.

"Oh, uh . . . sorry," I muttered as casually as I could, taking my hands away from my ears.

Will squinted at me. "Are you okay, Sven? You're acting kinda weird."

I rubbed my eyes with my palms. "I'm fine," I said quickly, even though I seriously doubted that was true. "I guess I'm just . . . tired from getting the oil earlier. Sorry."

Alicia's eyes bored into me. "No, you're not. It's the voice again, isn't it?"

"No, no," I insisted. "Like I said, I'm just tired. I haven't heard the voice in, like, forever." I hated lying to her, but I couldn't stand the idea of having some big discussion about the voice in my head. I already knew how different I was. How weird I was. I couldn't stomach the thought of sitting around discussing yet another way I was a freak. I thought I had found friends who accepted me as I was. But would they once they learned about the angry thoughts and escalating demands that shrilled in my head?

Or was it already too late? The way Alicia was looking

at me . . . Was that a hint of distrust in her eyes? I shook my head, trying to dislodge the black thoughts that were taking root there.

The voice had faded away. But it left an echo of unease in its wake. Maybe they were all plotting to kill me at the first opportunity.

Will wouldn't stop staring at me. Was that concern on his face? Or revulsion? Sure, we both had our . . . little quirks that set us apart from the "normal" kids at school. And we had been best friends forever. But who knew? Now I was probably too messed up even for him. He and Alicia were probably going to do something as soon as I turned my back, because they hated me. *I know they hate me. I can't trust them. I can only trust the Ticks because they're the only family I . . .*

Wait! *STOP!* What was I thinking? This was exactly what the voice wanted. I needed to shake myself out of it!

I grabbed two handfuls of my hair and yanked hard. *Snap out of it, Sven! Don't think this way! They're your friends. They really, really are! And you're their friend. Nothing the voice says can change that! Nothing!*

Everyone was still staring at me like I had two heads.

"You can't fool me, Sven," Alicia said gently. "But if it's the voice, it's okay. I know you're not going to hurt us."

"Hurt us?" Will asked, flicking the window latch open and closed. "What are you talking about, Alicia? What voice?"

I met her eyes with a silent plea.

She shook her head sadly. "I have to tell them, Sven."

"Tell us what?" Will demanded.

"Sven . . . sometimes hears a voice. He thinks someone might be . . . trying to hack into his mind. So they can get him to stop us."

"What?" Will paled. "Sven, is that true?"

I sighed. "Fine. I've been . . . hearing a voice. In my head."

Will laughed. "Oh, ppssshhhh. That's it? What's the big deal? I hear a voice in my head all the time. It's an OCD thing. It tells me that if I don't do certain things, something bad will happen. Like *If you don't check to see if there's an earthworm in that lasagna, there will be an earthworm in that lasagna*. It's fine, Sven."

I shook my head. "It's not like that. I'm actually hearing a real voice. And it's . . . it's getting louder."

"Hold on." Dix raised his eyebrows. "You're saying someone's trying to hack into your brain? I haven't been hearing any voices. And I'm a Tick, just like you."

"Me neither," Ivy added. "Nobody's trying to mess with my brain. If they did, I'd kick their butt!"

Alicia looked at her. "You're sure?"

"Of course I'm sure," Ivy huffed. "You think I wouldn't know if I suddenly started hearing voices?"

"So why would Sven be the only one hearing it?" Dix asked.

I shrugged. "I don't know. I'm the seventh and last Omicron they made. Maybe they gave me the special voices-in-your-head upgrade package?"

Will laughed nervously.

"Well, whatever the reason," Alicia said, her face grim, "I bet it has something to do with the kid who took down the Internet and his twin. The sooner we find them, the sooner we can stop them. Sam, how long until we get there?"

"We've just passed Spokane," 808 called back from the dashboard. "We should get to Seattle in a little under four hours."

Alicia fished the remaining throwing stars out of her backpack and checked that the magnets glued to them were still secure. "We don't know what we're going to find when we get there. So let's rest up. It's been a long trip, and we need to be ready for a fight."

Everyone nodded.

Then the only sound was the low thrum of the tires on the asphalt and the whistle of wind through the RV's broken window.

I leaned back and closed my eyes, but the torrent of worries whirling around in my head made it impossible to sleep. As I sat there fretting, something warm and wet slapped against the side of my face.

It was Thor's tongue. The dog studied me with his intelligent brown eyes and nuzzled under my arm with a reassuring grunt. The soft warmth of his fur was comforting. I rested my head against his side, and soon the manic thoughts subsided, replaced by the calming sound of Thor's heartbeat. Still, I didn't think there was much chance of getting to sleep.

"Wake up, kids!" Sam prompted. "Look! The Space Needle!"

I blinked and rubbed the sleep out of my eyes, then looked out the window. There, jutting up prominently in front of a gray skyline, stood the futuristic landmark.

I swallowed down a mix of emotions. We were in Seattle! And that meant we were closing in on the butt that took down the Internet.

I thought of the scorpipedes that flooded out of Bing's mouth. Roz's lethal tentacles. And yet, I knew what we might find in Seattle could be worse than either of those things.

Another thought brought my spirits even lower. *What if we can't find them at all?*

We had a whole city to search. And the world was already falling apart without the Internet. I heard an angry shout from outside and looked through the window in time to see two men near an out-of-order ATM swinging at each other.

"Don't worry, Sven." Alicia must have noticed my bleak expression. "We'll find them."

Her optimism was oddly contagious, because I found the muscles at the corners of my mouth reversing my frown. Or maybe it was just relief that Alicia really did seem to believe in me, in spite of the murderous soundtrack that kept churning through my mind.

"You know," I began, "you might just be right about that."

And then, as if somehow the Fates sensed that this would be a perfect time to pull the rug right out from under me, the smell of burning motor home assaulted my nose.

CHAPTER 33.0:

\ < value= [I Give Sam a Knuckle Sandwich] \ >

ACRID SMOKE, THICK AND SUFFOCATING as a wet wool blanket, filled the vehicle.

"Get out!" someone yelled.

I leapt up and groped my way toward the door. I might as well have been swimming in an acid sea at midnight. I was totally blind, my eyes tearing in response to the hot smoke scraping across the surface of my corneas.

"Hey, boss," 808 chirped in my ear. "Just a suggestion—maybe we should get out of here. You know, so we can keep living and whatnot."

My hand managed to close around the door handle. I twisted it and tumbled to the pavement. Once I could breathe again, I got to my feet and looked around. Sprawled on the sidewalk were Will, Dix, Sam, and Thor.

But where are Ivy and Alicia?

"Alicia!" I screamed. "Ivy!"

For several long seconds, there was no response. My blood thundered in my ears.

Then . . .

Movement in the RV's doorway.

Alicia stumbled out of the motor home with Ivy slung over her shoulder. She slumped to the ground. "Is Ivy okay?" she choked out between coughs.

I lifted Ivy and carried her clear of the burning vehicle.

"Ivy!" I called. "Ivy! Can you hear me? Are you all right?"

Her head bobbed up and down. "I'm okay," she croaked. Her blue eyes, bloodshot from the smoke, looked up at me. "Thanks for saving me, big bro."

I shook my head. "I didn't save you."

"Then who . . ."

"Her seat belt wouldn't open," Alicia said shakily. "I had to cut her free."

"*You* saved me, Alicia?" Ivy whispered. "But I thought you hated me."

Alicia shrugged. "*Hate* is a strong word, but . . . well, you're one of us, Ivy. And even if you're one of the most annoying, pain-in-the-butt kids I've ever met in my entire life, we're in this together."

Ivy wiped away a tear that snaked down her soot-stained cheek. "That's the nicest thing anybody's ever said to me." After a few deep breaths, she added, "But if you expect me to stop being an annoying pain in the butt, you're stupider than you look." She squinted balefully at Alicia for effect, but couldn't conceal the affectionate little gleam in her eyes.

"Is everyone unhurt?" Sam interrupted.

"Yeah," Ivy replied, getting to her feet. "What happened?"

Sam, his face flushed, looked at the sidewalk, and scratched the back of his neck. "Um . . . I guess . . . maybe the . . . gas tank, um . . . ruptured," he mumbled.

"Hey!" Ivy argued. "I thought you said that wasn't going to happen!"

Sam bit his lip and grimaced. "Sorry."

"So what do we do?" Dix asked.

"We walk," Alicia said resolutely. "Let's go."

She strode off in the direction of the distant Space Needle without a glance back.

We walked almost five blocks before anyone broke the silence.

"I'm concerned," Sam muttered.

I let out a flat laugh. "Really? Let me guess. It has something to do with the fact Ticks are trying to kill everyone on Earth and our only chance of stopping them depends on us finding one kid somewhere in a city with hundreds of thousands of people in it, right?"

"Actually, no," Sam responded. "I was thinking about my equipment. Now that it's gone up in flames . . . What if we have to access your CPU again? Or Dixon's or Thor's or Ivy's?"

I shrugged. "Why would you have to? We stopped Dix's performance. Ivy is, like, a thousand miles away from the Cheyenne Mountain Complex, so I don't see her starting World War III. And Thor? Without Dr. Schlumpf giving him commands, he's just a big puppy. He wouldn't . . . Wait. You're not worried about them, are you? You're worried about *me*. You think the voice is going to take me over or something?"

Sam frowned at me. "All I'm saying is maybe we could have modified your code to shut out anyone trying to hack into you."

"You still don't see me as a person, do you? I'm just a piece of technology to you! Something you can experiment on!"

And in that flash of anger, the voice spoke. *Hit him, Sven.*

Before I realized what was happening, my right fist shot out and slammed into Sam's jaw. He stumbled backward and tripped over the curb, falling gracelessly to the sidewalk.

Instantly, the fiery anger that had flooded my body was gone. All that was left was a crushing sense of guilt.

"I'm so sorry, Sam!" I cried. "I didn't mean to do that!"

Alicia darted over and twisted my arm behind my back. "Why did you do that, Sven?" she hissed.

"I . . . I . . . I don't know. It was like I wasn't in control of myself. I . . ."

Sam rubbed his jaw and stared at me. After a long moment, he spoke. "It's okay. No permanent damage." He got to his feet. "But I think this underscores the importance of finding the Tick that's hiding out here in Seattle as fast as we can. He's a next-level hacker. It's reasonable to think he might be the one accessing Sven's brain."

"Can I let you go, Sven?" Alicia asked. "Or are you going to do something stupid again?"

I nodded. "I think I'm okay now. I'm sorry. I don't know what happened."

Alicia let go of my arm. I rubbed the pain out of my shoulder. By then, Ivy, Will, Dix, and Thor had joined us and were looking at me like I was radioactive. I couldn't meet their eyes.

"Listen, guys." Will put his hand on my shoulder. "Whatever is going on with my best friend, we're going to stop it, okay? All we need to do is find the kid with the butt."

"You're right," Dix sighed. "But we still don't know how."

Ivy nodded somberly. "Well, I guess we'd better keep going, then."

We all nodded and continued making our way toward the Space Needle.

The hilliness of Seattle didn't make our walk particularly fun. When we weren't slogging uphill, we were shambling downhill. By the time we had trudged another half dozen blocks, drops of sweat were running down my forehead. They gathered on the tip of my nose before plopping to the sidewalk.

We were halfway down a particularly steep hill when Will shuffled to a halt and leaned against a tree. "Let's stop for a minute, okay? I'm wiped."

I opened my mouth to respond, but I didn't have the chance. Because a city bus screeched around the corner and came barreling right toward me.

CHAPTER 34.0:

\ < value= [Bus Stop] \ >

I DOVE TO THE GROUND. THE BUS PASSED so close by that its slipstream ruffled my hair. I looked up just in time to see it plow into a row of parked cars.

"Sven!" Will and Alicia cried in unison, rushing over to where I sprawled on the sidewalk.

Alicia leaned in close. "Are you okay?"

"Yeah," I replied, slowly sitting up. "I'm all right."

Will extended his hand and helped me to my feet.

"We need to check on the people in that bus!" Dixon yelled over his shoulder, already sprinting toward the wreck. "They might be hurt!"

He pried the doors open and disappeared inside. By

the time we got to the bus, Dix was helping the driver down the steps. She looked shaken up, but unharmed.

"Oh my gosh!" The driver looked at me with concern. "Are you okay? I . . . I ran out of gas. The power steering went out just as I was making the turn and I lost control. I was hoping I had enough fuel to make it to the depot. I'm so sorry!"

"It's fine," I told her. "You missed me."

She let out a relieved sigh. "Thank goodness!"

"What about your passengers?" Will asked.

"No passengers," she replied. "I wasn't picking up, just getting back to home base. Call came over from dispatch. The electricity just went out everywhere. I heard the whole country is in the dark."

"Electricity has been cut too?" Sam asked, scratching his chin fretfully. "It's getting worse. He's disabling key infrastructure. Who knows how long it'll be before we fall into complete civil unrest?"

As if on cue, a series of angry shouts echoed through the mostly deserted streets. They were silenced by what sounded like a gunshot.

Ivy pointed to the driver. "Maybe she can help. She drives a bus. She probably knows every inch of this city."

"Seriously?" Alicia scoffed. "'Excuse me, but we're looking for a kid with a butt who lives in Seattle.' I have a feeling no matter how well she knows the city, she can't help."

The woman laughed. "Well, you're right there. I can't say I know which kid with a butt you're talking about. A lot of kids have them these days. Besides, the only part of this city I know every inch of is my route. That's all I've been driving since I took this job three years ago."

She extended her thumb toward the back of the bus, where her route information was displayed on an illuminated sign over the rear window.

QUEEN ANNE AVE N & W ALOHA ST

A thought in the very back of my mind stirred to life. There was something about that sign. . . . *What is it?* I whispered the words aloud, turning them over in my head, trying to make the connection.

Aloha.

What was it about the word *aloha*?

And then it clicked.

"Sam!" I exclaimed. "The limerick!"

He scratched his tangled nest of hair. "What?"

"The limerick! The one that was embedded in the source code of the butt picture! You copied it down! Do you still have the paper?"

He nodded uncertainly. "Oh, that? Yes, I think so. Hold on. . . ."

After he produced it from his pocket, I smoothed it out on my thigh.

there once was a butt like a STar
whose owner was bound to go far
ALOHA, he said
you'll all soon be dead
in the WEST I am called chapeau noir

"Look! *Aloha!*" I held the paper up for my friends to see.

Ivy frowned at me. "I don't get it."

"It says *aloha* on the bus, too!" I explained.

"And?" Alicia said. "It's a Hawaiian greeting. Probably just a coincidence."

"Yeah, well, is it a coincidence that it also says *west*?"

"Maybe," Alicia countered, a little less certainly.

I gestured to the bus again. "And what about the fact that the first two letters of star are capitalized? *ST*, like 'street'!"

"Wait! West Aloha Street!" Dixon cried excitedly. "Sven, I think you might be onto something here!"

Thor nuzzled my hand encouragingly.

Will blinked at me. "No way! You're saying you think that hacker put the name of his street in that limerick? Seriously, dude? Why the heck would he do that?"

"It's like an Easter egg," Sam suggested. "A hidden joke or clue. Back when my team and I were working to develop the early AI used by the Ticks, we were always hiding little inside jokes in the code. We figured no one would ever find them. Whoever hid that limerick in the source code was probably doing the same thing."

"I don't know . . . ," Alicia mused. "This kid's smart

enough to take down the whole Internet, but he's stupid enough to leave a clue like this?"

I nodded. "That's just it. He probably thinks he's smarter than everybody. I bet he counted on no one being able to figure it out."

"Well, he has a point," 808 remarked. "Humans do tend to be . . . how can I put this delicately? Dumb as a box of rocks."

Ivy turned to the bus driver. "Can you tell us where West Aloha Street is?"

"Just head up that way about, oh . . . twelve blocks or so. Turn left on Mercer, right on Queen Anne, and you'll run right into West Aloha on your left. It's just a block long, so you should have a good chance of finding what you're looking for." She peered at me. "You sure I didn't clip you there? I think I'm supposed to report it when I hit people with the bus. But it's so much paperwork."

I nodded. "Believe me, I'm fine."

"All right, then," she said. "Good luck with that butt."

* * *

It was early evening by the time we reached West Aloha Street. The sun was hanging low, throwing slanting shafts of light through the trees. Even though it wasn't quite dark yet, a sort of gloom hung in the air.

The streets were practically empty.

We made our way along West Aloha Street, scanning every building for anything out of the ordinary. Most of the structures were apartment buildings, anywhere from two to six stories high. I sighed. West Aloha might only have been one block, but that didn't mean it was going to be easy to find what we were looking for.

Will picked up a twig and started tapping it seven times against every tree and telephone pole we passed. "I hope we find this place soon. With the power out, we're going to be searching for it in the pitch dark before long."

"My feet hurt," Ivy complained. "What are we even looking for, anyway?"

"Just anything that doesn't look right," Alicia responded.

"What about that, chief?" From my shoulder, 808 pointed half a dozen legs toward a little statue in front of one of the buildings. It was a garden gnome sitting on a little toilet reading a newspaper. "That *definitely* doesn't look right."

"Maybe not." Sam chuckled. "But I don't think that's what we're looking for."

Will looked pale in the fading light. "We're not going to find him, are we?"

No one answered.

By the time we reached the end of the street, we hadn't seen any sign of a superhacker Tick programmed to destroy the world.

Until Dix stopped so abruptly, I walked right into his back.

"Look!" he cried, extending an arm toward a three-story brick building on the corner. "Do you see it? Right there!"

I looked eagerly to where he was pointing. That's when I saw . . .

CHAPTER 35.0:
\ < value= [Monkey Business [Literally]] \ >

. . . ABSOLUTELY NOTHING.

I squinted toward the building. It was made of red brick with white trim and black shutters. The front yard consisted of a small patch of grass encircled by a chain-link fence. A blue minivan sat in the driveway. "I don't see anything."

"Yeah," Ivy added. "It's just a house."

He jogged to the building and gestured toward a little button to the right of the door.

"Um . . . Dix, that's a doorbell." Will shrugged. "You might not realize this because you're, like, famous, and so you're probably used to staying in hotels and stuff, but most houses have them. You see, you push the button and it goes *ding-dong* so the people inside know there's someone at the door—"

Dix cut him off. "I know what a doorbell is, man. But *look* at the doorbell!"

It took a second for me to realize what he was talking about. Then it hit me. The button was illuminated. "Wait! They have electricity?"

Dix placed his hands on his hips and nodded. "Looks like it. The whole city is in the dark except this one house on West Aloha Street? Seems kinda significant to me."

"It is. And that's not all," Sam added. He nodded toward a tall cell phone transmission tower right next to the building. "See that? There's a cable leading from that tower to a window on the third floor."

Alicia slid her knife out of her backpack and clipped the sheath to the waist of her pants. "Okay, looks like we found it!"

Before anyone could even begin formulating a plan, she dashed up the steps and joined Dixon on the porch.

She pounded on the front door, ready to leap into action, her knees bent, her fingers arched like talons.

After several agonizing seconds, during which I imagined a whole range of nightmare-inducing Ticks, a light came on in the front hallway. The door swung open. A wedge of warm electric light cast its glow onto the dusky porch.

A shape was silhouetted against the light spilling from the building. It was short. It looked kind of human. It was . . .

"A monkey!" Dix squealed. "It's a monkey! Oh my gosh, it's a *monkey*!" He scooped the little primate up in his arms and cackled with delight.

"Oh, I see you've already met Oscar," a woman's voice said from inside the house. "He loves company. Won't you come in?"

I cautiously climbed the steps with Thor at my side. Will, Ivy, and Sam were right behind us. Alicia stood motionless on the porch. Her hand rested on the hilt of her knife, but she hadn't removed the blade from its sheath. I could tell from her posture that she was confused. But when Dix eagerly strode into the house, she shrugged and followed him inside.

I entered right on her heels.

The first thing I noticed was the wallpaper. It was printed with a repeating pattern of palm trees and coconuts. As far as I could tell, it covered every wall in the place. The second thing I noticed was a middle-aged woman sitting in a wheelchair, dressed in a floral-print dress that clashed with the walls. She had a warm, friendly face and a welcoming smile. Salt-and-pepper hair was piled atop her head in a loose bun. Her red horn-rimmed glasses perched happily on the bridge of her nose.

"Well, it's nice to finally meet you," she said, extending a hand to Sam.

Sam cautiously shook her hand. "You were . . . you were expecting us?"

"Of course," the woman replied. "I'm Janet Ito. And you're here to pick up Oscar, right?"

"Yes!" Dix enthused. "Yes, we are!"

Sam shook his head. "Actually, no. I'm afraid I don't understand. Do you give away monkeys to everyone who comes to your door?"

Janet Ito laughed. "No, we don't give away monkeys to just anyone. You have to go through a rigorous application process. You see, I train helper monkeys."

Ivy asked, "What are helper monkeys?"

"They're service animals that have been taught to help people who are visually impaired, have difficulty with mobility, have lost the use of their hands, or are dealing with other disabilities. My husband, Seiji, and I train them. We like to call this Monkey University."

"Monkey University?" Dixon's eyes lit up. "Wait! Does that mean you have *more* monkeys?"

"Oh, yes," Janet replied. "At any given time, we usually have about eight monkeys in training. I wish we could take on more, but getting them ready for placement takes a tremendous amount of work. About three or four years of classes on following commands and doing household chores and . . . well, answering the door like Oscar just did."

"You're a good boy, aren't you, Oscar?" Dix told the monkey.

Oscar nodded and pinched Dix's nose.

"So, if you're not here for Oscar, what can I help you

with?" the woman asked. "Oh, no. You're not here about Mi, are you?"

I blinked at her. "Are we here about *you*?"

She shook her head. "No, not 'me.' *Mi.* Mitsuo Tanaka. He's always getting into trouble on that computer of his. Do you know what he did last month? He somehow hacked into the data the Mars explorer was transmitting back to Earth and made the scientists at NASA think there was an alien on Mars mooning them."

"Mooning them?" I shot Alicia a knowing glance, then continued. "Who exactly is Mitsuo?"

The woman's friendly smile disappeared instantly. She glanced up the staircase behind her, then turned back to us with a frown. "Who are you people? Why are you here?"

The room fell silent as we struggled for something to tell her. I picked up Alicia's tension as she trained her eyes on the staircase.

I knew the look on her face. She was going to do something. And it would probably result in injury or destruction. Or, I thought with a shudder, maybe both.

CHAPTER 36.0:

\ < value= [Working. Shut Up. Kthanksbye.] \ >

BEFORE ALICIA COULD PUT HER PLAN into action, Dix spoke up. "Don't worry. We're just here because Mitsuo Tanaka is the grand-prize winner!" He waved his hands in the air excitedly to accentuate the point.

A look of confusion passed over Janet Ito. "What are you talking about?"

Dix turned up the charm even more. "You don't recognize me, do you? I'm Dixon Watts. And Mitsuo Tanaka entered the *Go on Tour with Dixon* contest. We drew his name at random from over a million entries. And he won! So my crew and I are here to take him backstage for my next show. With your permission, of course."

For a moment, the woman just stared at him. "You're pulling my leg," she said at last. "You're *not* Dixon Watts! If you are, let's hear you sing."

My stomach dropped somewhere down to the region of my ankles.

But before I could even think about stopping him . . .

Girl, you are my scrambled eggs.
I love you and your bacon legs!

To me, of course, it sounded like a cat coughing up a hairball. But Janet Ito must have heard something else entirely. Her face lit up. So did Alicia's, Will's, and Sam's. They all looked at Dix like he was some kind of musical god.

"Yikes," 808 whispered into my ear. "What the heck is that noise coming out of the hole in his face?"

"It's true! You really are him!" Janet Ito leapt up from the wheelchair and threw her arms around Dix. "That was amazing!"

"Whoa, whoa, *whoa*!" Ivy cried. "What the heck?

That no-talent eardrum mangler can make people in wheelchairs walk again?"

Janet laughed. "No, no. The wheelchair is a prop. I use it to help with the monkeys' training so they get used to working with wheelchair-bound people. But . . . I can't believe it's really you! Mitsuo and his sister, Yuki, are going to be so excited. Ever since I've fostered them, I've wanted to treat them to something really special. You should go right up and surprise them. They're on the third floor. Oscar can show you where it is. They'll just flip!"

"Thank you, Ms. Ito." Dix gently pried her arms from around his neck. "I'm excited to meet them too."

"Oscar, guests . . . kids' room," she instructed the monkey, speaking slowly and clearly.

With a happy *eek eek*, Oscar took Dixon's hand and led the way up the stairs.

The second floor of the house was filled with toys, boxes, and other items that must have been used to train the monkeys. Not to mention the nearly overpowering stench of monkey.

There were seven of them on the second floor, each

pretty much identical to Oscar. Maybe two feet tall and covered with brown fur, they had pale faces with tufts of hair that sat atop their heads like fuzzy little hats.

They had been playing noisily as we climbed the stairs. But as we emerged onto the second floor, they froze and fell silent. Seven pairs of big, brown, too-human eyes locked onto us and tracked our progress down the hall.

Dix grinned at the creatures and waved excitedly.

My skin prickled with unease. There was something unsettling about being watched by creatures that were so close to being human but weren't actually human.

I tore my gaze away from them and hurried to the stairs that led up to the top floor. Oscar led us down a short hallway to a closed door. He reached up, twisted the doorknob, and pushed the door open.

We walked into a room that looked pretty much like any kids' room. Books, dirty clothes, and empty food wrappers covered the floor. Two unmade beds were pushed up against opposite walls. Two matching desks sat side by side facing a pair of windows.

And that's where we found a boy and a girl—Mitsuo and Yuki Tanaka.

They were sitting with their backs to us. The boy, Mitsuo, was hunched over a computer keyboard, while Yuki just stared intently out the window.

I cleared my throat. "Um, hi! Yuki? Mitsuo? My name is Sven. These are my friends. And we—"

"Shhh!" the boy hissed. "I'm busy!"

I tried again. "I know you're busy, but this is really important. The whole world is—"

"Don't care," he snapped, not even sparing a glance in our direction. "Shut up. Kthanksbye."

"But we need your help!" Alicia demanded. Then she added in a very un-Alicia-like way, "*Please*."

Mitsuo slammed his fist down on his desk. "If you don't leave right—"

"Mi," the girl interrupted without turning from the window. "Don't be rude."

"Fine, I can go AFK for precisely three minutes." Mitsuo spun around to face us, brushing his straight black hair out of his eyes. "What do you want? Go."

Three minutes wasn't a lot of time to explain to someone that they were a Synthetic programmed to wipe out everyone on the planet.

I tried to find a way to broach the subject. "Um . . . you see . . . uh . . . you're not what you think you are. You're . . . um . . . really not human kids. Well, not . . . you know . . . the kind of normal human kid that most normal human kids are . . . not that I'm saying you're abnormal, of course . . . it's just—"

"Is this about us being androids?" Mitsuo snapped. "Old news. Tell me something I don't know. Ticktock, now you have two minutes."

CHAPTER 37.0:
\ < value= [Things Are Totally Horked] \ >

"WH-WH-WHAT?" I STUTTERED. "YOU *KNOW* about that?"

Mitsuo rolled his eyes at me. "Why wouldn't I? It's kind of obvious."

"Hold on!" Dix gaped at him. "Are you saying you've always known? You never thought you were human?"

The boy laughed. "Geez, you guys aren't so bright, are you?"

"Mi, be nice," Yuki said, finally spinning around to face us. She reached out a fluttering hand to touch her brother's shoulder. "They're like us."

It was then I realized she hadn't been looking out the

window. She hadn't been looking at anything at all. Her eyes were pure white. No iris. No pupil. She was blind.

Mitsuo scowled. "What are you talking about? No one's like us!"

"They are, brother." She stared sightlessly ahead. "These two are Seven and Six Omicron. The dog is Four. And the little one is Five."

"It's Ivy, thank you very much," Ivy snapped.

"I'm sorry," Yuki said gently. "I'm being rude. We've never met anyone like us before. I apologize for reading you."

I blinked at her. "What do you mean?"

Yuki paused before speaking. "You think I'm blind. Well, that's partly true. I can't see shapes and colors. Or people's faces. I've never seen a flower. But I *can* see. Just not the same way you do. I see circuitry and wire. Programming and code. When I'm close to a device, I see everything that makes it function. And if Mitsuo gives me the code, I can control it. Whether it's a toaster or a computer or an ATM . . . or an android like you. So, to answer your question, I can read your names in your coding. I can read all about you."

"So that's why you've always known what you were," Alicia said. "You could read it in yourself."

Yuki nodded. "We always thought we were the only ones like us." She smiled. "But it's good to know we're not alone."

"Perhaps we should discuss why we're here," Sam suggested.

Mitsuo glared at him. "Why *are* you here? We're busy."

"Yeah, we know." Will sat down on one of the beds. "You're the ones who took down the Internet. And the whole country's electrical grid."

"You're welcome," Mitsuo replied with a smug grin.

Sam raised his eyebrows. "I must admit, it's impressive. I assume you infiltrated the Internet backbone through a core router at a central node and shut it down."

"Don't insult me," Mitsuo snorted. "A central node? Sure, that could take down part of the Internet. For a little while. But that's like trying to swim up a waterfall. That's how a noob who wants to get caught might do it. Not me. Look."

He pointed out the window to the cell tower that we had noticed from the street. "You know how many smartphones there are in the world? More than two *billion*! They're all over the place! Everywhere! Which means you crack into them and you have two billion decentralized micronodes that can feed whatever you want back into any network on Earth from two billion constantly moving places."

Whatever he was talking about was totally over my head. But Sam nodded knowingly. "That's pretty smart. But how could you possibly get into two billion encrypted smartphones worldwide?"

"That's where I come in," Yuki told him. "My brother didn't access those phones. I did. He wrote the code that brought down the Internet and the electric grid. But I provided the key to unlocking all those phones to put that code into play. We're a team."

"Bravo." Alicia leaned in close to him and spoke in a soft but threatening voice. "Now *undo* it. Bring the Internet back. The power grid. Everything. Fix it all. Right now."

"Fix it?" Mitsuo cried. "What are you talking about? I *am* fixing it! Because it was all already broken. The whole system! Arbitrary power in the hands of a dishonest government, backed by their armies and their laws, which can be selectively ignored by those who have money or connections while the rest of us are trodden underfoot! We all need to be free! Free from their shackles, their laws! Free from the economy that's designed to keep us enslaved by the almighty dollar. It all has to be torn down!"

I flinched at the intensity of his words. "You're talking about anarchy."

"Call it anarchy if you want. I call it equality! Justice! Freedom! What we're doing is making things right!"

"What you're doing," Alicia growled, "is destroying civilization."

"Yeah, right. Civilization! You mean imprisonment. How can we be free if we have to live within a system that gives the corrupt few unchecked power over the many?"

"These guys are nuts," 808 whispered in my ear. "I

mean, can you imagine a world where money is worthless? What would you use to buy frozen yogurt? Madness!"

Alicia slid her knife out of its sheath. "I'm going to say it one more time. Then things are going to get messy. Put everything back to the way it was."

"If you're trying to scare me, it won't work. Hurt me and nobody will be able to unwind my code. It'd take a whole army of computer experts months, maybe years, to get things back to normal. What do you think will happen to the world while you wait? No power. No Internet. Transportation is totally horked. So do what you want. I've already won."

I looked at the gleam in his eye. Did he even know that he was just a tool the Ticks were using to wipe out humanity?

Alicia hefted the knife in her hand and stepped toward the boy. "I'll get you to put things right! Even if I have to persuade you one bloody chunk at a time."

"Stop." I put my hand on her shoulder. "He's right. He's already won."

Mitsuo smiled. "I'm glad you finally get it."

"Oh, I do," I told him. "You've done a great job. Your overseer must be very pleased."

Mi shook his head. "Overseer?"

"Sure. All Omicrons have overseers. They make sure we carry out our instructions properly. I had Dr. Shallix. Dixon had Roz. Ivy had Bing. Before we got rid of them. So who's yours?"

"We don't have one," he replied with a tilt of his head.

I laughed. "Of course you do. That's how it works. If you deviate from your programming, they step in and—"

"My programming?" Mitsuo said, his face reddening. "I'm doing what I'm doing because it's right, not because someone . . . programmed me to do it."

"Okay, you can believe that little fantasy if you want. You might think you're acting on your own free will to take down a corrupt system, but the truth is, you're just doing what they told you to do. The Ticks. The ones who created us. We're just tools they're using to take over the planet."

Mitsuo's hands clenched into fists. "Not true!"

Dixon stepped to my side. "It is, man. He's telling the truth."

Even 808 jumped in. "He ain't lyin', kid. I was part of an overseer. Well, they made me live in the little toe and I didn't get to do much, but take it from me, it's all true."

"You definitely have an overseer." I turned to Yuki. "Let me ask you, is Janet Ito a Tick? Or her husband? Maybe they're your overseers."

Yuki shook her head. "They're human. I can't read them." A worried expression crossed her face. "But . . ."

"But what?" I asked.

"But me," a voice said behind us.

I looked toward the doorway to find its source.

It was Oscar.

CHAPTER 38.0:
\< value= [This Is Worse Than *Planet of the Apes*] \>

IT TOOK A MOMENT FOR MY BRAIN TO click into gear. Monkeys didn't usually talk. And his voice was so deep, it was hard to believe it came from an animal that barely reached my kneecap.

"Oh my . . . oh my . . . oh my *gosh*!" Dix gushed. "He can talk! That's so awesome! Look, guys, Oscar can talk!"

I didn't think it was so awesome. But then again, I had seen *Planet of the Apes* a few months earlier, and it totally freaked me out.

Dix kneeled down and grinned at Oscar. "Hey there, little fella," he cooed.

Instead of answering, Oscar raised his arms toward

Dix's face. As I watched, the monkey's fingers fused into two huge ragged claws that looked like they should have been scuttling across the floor of silent seas—not attached to the end of a primate. Brown and hard, they were clad in the kind of thick, unforgiving armor that protected a lobster. And they were much larger than you would have expected monkey claws to be.

WHOOSH SNAP!

One of Oscar's claws arced down toward Dix's face, the serrated edges slamming together with such force, it sounded like someone had set off a firecracker.

Okay, so it wasn't just *Planet of the Apes*. This was definitely not cool!

Dix, who had been leaning in, was luckily spared the full effect of the attack. The side of the pincer connected with his cheekbone and sent him sprawling on the floor.

"He's a Tick!" Alicia screamed. She dove for her backpack.

"I believe the plural would be more accurate," Oscar said with a sneer.

Right on cue, the other seven monkeys appeared. Each

had a pair of deadly-looking claws. They moved with frightening speed, using their prehensile tails to make up for the agility lost to their cross-species redesign.

Yuki stood up tentatively. "What's happening? Is that . . . ?"

"It's your dumb monkey," Ivy informed her. "Only he's not really a monkey. He's a Tick! They're all Ticks!"

"Indeed," Oscar admitted. "We replaced the organic simians here in the Itos' domicile just as you and your brother were fostered. Our job was to ensure you carried out your mission at the appropriate time. You performed admirably. Until these humans and Synthetic traitors decided to interfere. We cannot let them get in the way of your mission."

"There you go," 808 piped up. "Kids, meet your overseers."

"Oscar? But—but why couldn't I read you?" Yuki stammered.

The monkey laughed. "We'd be pretty poor overseers if you knew we were overseeing you. Especially given your rebellion algorithms. We were extra careful to keep our defenses up around you, my dear Yuki. So you couldn't access our programming. But enough about us. You and Mitsuo still have a chance to survive. We will let you live if you continue to carry out your mission and dismantle all human infrastructure as instructed."

"Oh, so you mean just follow orders, is that it?" Mitsuo said with a sneer. "What do you think our answer is, maggotbox?"

"A shame." Oscar shook his head. "I had been hoping you'd be eager to join those of us who are committed to furthering the Synthetic cause. But you sound less than enthusiastic at the prospect of—"

"Hey, catch!"

Alicia heaved a magnetic throwing star at Oscar. It whooshed across the room, a silver streak of pointy-toothed steel. But when it reached its target, the monkey raised a claw and snatched it out of the air.

Two neatly cut pieces of star clattered to the floor.

"You know, she really shouldn't have said, 'Hey, catch' before she threw that," 808 whispered in my ear. "Totally lost the element of surprise."

"If you've finished playing around with your toys . . ."

Oscar sighed. The eight monkeys advanced on us, claws raised.

Thor leapt in front of me and growled at them. As they closed in, he lunged forward, snapping his jaws on one of the small brown torsos. He shook the creature like a stuffed dog toy and flung it across the room. It hit the wall with a *thud* and landed on the floor in a heap.

It took only a second or two for the little Tick to get back to its feet and pick up where it had left off, charging forward with pincers clacking.

We were in trouble. Alicia's knife attacks were useless against enemies with incomprehensibly fast reflexes. Every stab or slash was easily thwarted by an armored claw.

And she was the best among us at fighting. Will, Sam, Dix, Ivy, and I were basically hopeless. We ran this way and that trying to get away from our adversaries, but there were simply too many of them.

Ivy screamed as Oscar latched his pincer onto her wrist, scoring a bloody gouge in her flesh.

"No!" I snarled. "Leave her alone!"

I kicked at him as hard as I could, but he stepped aside and my foot only made contact with the empty air. The monkey grinned as I crashed to the floor.

Before I could even blink, his free claw shot out and closed around my throat.

"Filthy human," he spat. "Prepare to die. Any—"

The room suddenly disappeared in an intense white flash that made my retinas burn and sting. My head felt as if someone had plugged a high-pressure water hose directly into my skull. There were no more monkeys. No Alicia. No Will. No Dix. Nothing. Just whiteness all around. Slowly, a shape materialized in front of me. It was Yuki. She peered at me with large brown eyes—not the solid white ones I had seen just minutes earlier.

I couldn't tear my eyes from hers. They were so deep and knowing.

She must have noticed me staring, because she said, "You like them? I can try something else if you prefer."

She blinked, and her eyes went from brown to purple. "Or maybe this."

She blinked again, and a pair of orange eyes were facing me.

"I . . . I think I like the first ones best," I stammered.

"Me too," she replied, changing her eyes back to brown.

I looked around. Everything was so white and seamless, I couldn't tell if I was trapped in a tiny closet or a space that stretched on for miles in every direction. "What's happening? What did you do to me?"

"Don't worry," she assured me. "Nothing bad. I just wanted to have a little chat. So I popped over for a visit."

"Popped over? Where?"

Yuki laughed. "Into your brain. Or technically your CPU. I didn't want us to be interrupted, so I shut down your sensory processing subroutine."

I started to object, but she stopped me.

"Relax. You'll be as good as new in a minute. I just wanted to get a proper look at you. So, if you'll excuse me, I'm going to poke around a little."

"Hey, wait! What do you mean you're going to poke . . ."

She winked out of existence before I could finish the sentence.

"Yuki?" I called. "Yuki?"

There was no answer.

"Well, just don't break anything, okay?" I said.

And there I stood, all alone in my brain with nothing to do. Nothing to look at. No one to talk to. I tried humming aloud to amuse myself, but the hollow echo of my voice made me feel even more alone, so I stopped.

Finally, Yuki popped back.

She stared at me with a lopsided smile.

"Why are you looking at me like that?" I asked, trying to read the amused expression on her face.

Her smile broadened. "No reason. It's just that I checked out your memory storage." She stifled a laugh.

"What?"

"You tried to jump over a cake?" she snorted. "Seriously? Who jumps over a cake? And I also took just a tiny look at your emotion regulators. Did you know they're on the same circuit as your incursion defenses?"

"Um . . . no. My incursion defenses?"

Yuki nodded. "They're like a firewall. Your incursion defenses keep people from being able to access your system remotely. I mean, I can do it, obviously, because that's what I was designed to do. But the point is, because of the way you're built, when your emotion regulators are overclocked, your incursion defenses are at their weakest."

I tried to process what she was saying. "You mean when I'm emotional, I can be more easily . . . hacked?"

"You could put it that way."

"Is that why I hear a voice in my head when I'm angry or upset?" I asked.

Yuki scratched her chin. "Probably. Which brings me to the whole point of my visit. We need to do something about those monkeys. I need your help. If you can overtax their emotion regulators, I may be able to grab a piece of code from Mi, bypass their defenses, and disable them. Good luck!"

"Okay, but how exactly do I . . ."

Yuki disappeared.

A small dark spot rushed at me, growing larger

and larger until it formed itself into Yuki and Mitsuo's bedroom.

I lay pinned to the floor by Oscar just as I had been before Yuki drew me into my own head. The whole conversation with her had taken literally no time at all.

"—last words?" the Tick finished saying.

"Actually, yes," I said.

CHAPTER 39.0:

\ < value= [Mi Unhorks the Interwebs] \ >

I HAD NEVER BEEN VERY GOOD AT insulting people. I guess when you live your life with the nickname Trashmouth, you quickly realize how much being made fun of hurts. But if I wanted to survive for more than a few seconds, I needed to come up with a great insult fast!

I crossed my fingers and did my best. “Hey, anybody ever told you monkeys that you look like someone set your face on fire and put it out with an ugly stick?”

Oscar barely reacted. “Physical appearances are unimportant.”

Strike one. “Oh, uh . . . well, your mama’s a toaster!”

"Actually, my mother is a Synthetic Replicator, model 23-b. Now if there's nothing else . . ."

Uh-oh! "Wait!" I cried. "Um . . . it must be tough for stupid poop-flinging monkeys like you to fling poop with those big ugly claws of yours!"

The monkey blinked at me for a moment. Then his lips pulled back in a scowl. "How dare you!" he screamed. "I'll have you know our poop-flinging prowess is beyond reproach! I'll kill you slowly for that!"

"Mi," I heard Yuki shout. "They're overclocking! Get me some code for the monkeys!"

Oscar's claw slowly tightened around my throat.

"Got it, sis!" Mitsuo called out. "All yours!"

Suddenly, Oscar froze. All the monkeys froze. Then they toppled over, totally motionless.

I pushed Oscar off of me and got to my feet.

"Whoa!" Will nudged a deactivated monkey with the toe of his shoe. "What happened?"

"We scrogged those noobs!" Mitsuo crowed. "Used a modified rootkit to brick up their mobos!"

Dixon frowned. "Is that good?"

"They won't be bothering us again," Yuki explained.

Alicia cleared her throat. "I guess we owe you one. Now, about the damage you've done . . ."

Mitsuo sighed. "Yeah, yeah, fine. I'll make it right." He gestured at Oscar's inert form. "I can't believe we almost helped them wipe out humanity. What a bonehead I was."

"Fighting your programming isn't an easy thing to do, Mitsuo," Sam replied, scratching the gray stubble on his chin. "Ivy had an almost uncontrollable compulsion to sneak into the Cheyenne Mountain Complex to blow up the world. And Sven couldn't stop himself from eating the inedible, even though he wanted to."

Will chimed in. "And I have to lift the toilet seat up and down seven times before I pee."

Sam laughed. "See? Humans have their own programming too. But now that you know what's really going on, hopefully you and Yuki can fight it, if that's what you choose to do."

Mitsuo nodded.

After that, we stood without speaking, the only

sound in the room the rapid, staccato *clack clack clack* of Mi's fingers pressing keys.

"It's done," Mitsuo said after a while. "I unhorked the interwebs. And the power should come on any second now."

I looked out the window in time to see lights all over the city flicker on.

"Thank you," I said. "You did the right thing."

Mitsuo shrugged. "Good," he said, reverting back to his typical blunt self. "Now you can go. Bye."

Alicia used her knife to cut the cable running from Mitsuo's computer to the cell tower.

"Hey! Why'd you do that?"

"I'm not an idiot. You think I'm going to just let you bring down the Internet again?"

Mitsuo stood up. "I wasn't going to!"

"Forgive me if I don't take your word for it," Alicia replied coldly. "Now pack up some things if you want. We're leaving."

He blinked at her. "You want me to go with you?"

Will answered for her. "Until we've stopped all the Ticks, we figure it's safer having you and your sister with us. Just so you don't, you know, exterminate the human race as soon as our backs are turned."

"What if I don't want to go?"

Alicia fixed him with her cool green eyes. "You don't have to. But I don't think you'd like the alternative."

Mitsuo swallowed nervously. The threat in Alicia's voice was clear.

Yuki spoke for both of them. "Okay, fine. We'll go. But at least tell me where we're going."

Nobody answered her.

"You don't even know where you're going?" Mitsuo laughed. "Awesome! What could go wrong?"

"Anyone have any ideas?" I asked. "There's only one Tick left! We're so close!"

808 shrugged a few of his legs. "Don't look at me, boss."

"Actually, 808, you're exactly who I'm looking at."

"Can't help you. They've locked me out of the network," he objected.

I smiled. "True. But I think I know a couple of people who might be able to help. They're pretty good hackers."

* * *

"Los Angeles," 808 said once the Tanaka twins had restored his access to the network. "One Omicron is in LA. I've got an address: a building on Wilshire Boulevard. A company called Cyber Dynamics, Inc. Seventy-fifth floor. Fancy-schmancy."

Alicia turned toward the scorpipede. "What's his mission? Who's his overseer? What else can you tell us? I want to know everything."

"That'll be a problem," 808 told her. "I've told you all there is. Everything else in that particular file is blank."

Will flipped the light switch on and off. "That's not good."

"Know what's even worse?" Ivy interjected. "We have no way to get there. The RV must be a pile of ashes by now."

808 laughed. "Please. I've already taken care of it."

I squinted at him. "How have you taken—"

I was interrupted by the sound of a car horn outside.

CHAPTER 40.0:
\ < value= [Going Up] \ >

808 HADN'T JUST TAKEN CARE OF IT. HE had taken care of it in style! When we left the house, a huge, sleek, black limousine was waiting by the curb.

Will's jaw dropped. "Huh? How did you . . . ?"

The scorpipede chuckled from my shoulder. "While I was checking out Cyber Dynamics, I took the liberty of ordering us a car on their account. I hope they don't mind."

With big leather seats and a TV and snacks and soda, the limo was pretty much the polar opposite of Sam's RV. There were even pillows and blankets so we could get some sleep during the long drive to LA.

It was big enough to fit all of us with room to spare—even Yuki and Mitsuo, who had convinced Janet Ito to let them come along by promising they'd be in good hands with the famous and talented Dixon Watts. We were grateful to have room to stretch out a little, because after everything we'd been through recently, we totally needed sleep.

I had no idea how many hours I was out. But when I woke up, my nostrils stung with the stench of burning cars and tear gas.

I looked out the window and my stomach churned. Los Angeles was on fire. Plumes of thick, black smoke snaked up into the sky. Heavily armed police officers patrolled the streets, chasing masked rioters, shouting instructions through bullhorns.

"Yikes!" Will pressed his face to the window. "It's like a war zone!"

Dix gaped at the scene. "I was here just last week for a show. This looks like a different city altogether."

"Must have happened when the lights went out," Sam said. "When people don't have what they need, they tend to get violent."

Mitsuo's face reddened. "Oh, uh, yeah. Sorry about that. But, you know, no harm no foul, right?" He laughed nervously.

A group of three police officers stopped our limo. I watched as the driver, who hadn't spoken more than three words the entire trip, lowered his window and displayed some sort of identification.

"Cyber Dynamics," he growled.

One of the officers examined the ID, nodded, and waved us on.

The limo drove a few more blocks, then swung to the right. We paused in front of the entrance to a parking garage underneath a gleaming skyscraper.

"Whoa, snazzy!" Ivy remarked. "This is way bigger than anything in Colorado Springs."

The car rolled forward, and we plunged into semi-darkness as we entered the parking garage. Our driver stopped the limo right in front of a row of elevators. He opened our door and let us out. Then, with a tip of his hat, he climbed back into the limo and drove away.

We stood in front of a dozen elevator doors that

shone like polished mirrors. But it didn't take long for us to figure out it was the elevator on the end that we were looking for. It had an imposing pair of black doors and instead of a call button, a key-card reader. A small plaque above the device read:

CYBER DYNAMICS, INC.

"This is it," Alicia said, running her finger over the engraved letters on the plaque. "How do we get up?"

"Have you learned nothing, young padawan?" Mitsuo replied. "Yuki?"

"Connected." She nodded at her brother.

Mitsuo closed his eyes for a second. "Code in."

The doors whooshed open.

"Voilà." Mi gestured toward the empty car.

We filed into a sterile space lined in brushed steel. The walls, the floors, the ceiling were all wrapped in that seamless metal skin. Instead of a full set of buttons on the control panel, there were only two features—a key-card reader and a single button marked 75.

Mitsuo guided Yuki's hand to the button. It lit up, tinting the steel walls with a bloodred glow.

The elevator rose so smoothly and silently that the only indication we were moving at all was the mounting pressure on my eardrums.

A digital display counted the floors as we ascended.

Fourteen . . . fifteen . . . sixteen . . . seventeen . . .

It wasn't until we passed twenty-two that anybody spoke.

"So what's the plan?" Dix asked.

Ivy laughed. "I got a plan for you! We go in there and kick some butt!"

Thor whimpered and tucked his tail between his legs.

Ivy scratched his head. "Don't worry, boy. We got this!"

His tail popped up and wagged in response.

"Anyone heard of Cyber Dynamics before?" Will wondered aloud.

Alicia shook her head. "Nope. But don't worry. There's one more Tick to deal with and we're done. This is nearly over."

Will ran a finger under his nose thoughtfully. "Yeah, I guess." He sounded doubtful.

I patted him on the back. "It's going to be fine, Will. With all of us working together, we're going to do this!"

"Oh, right. Yeah, I know." Will nodded. But I couldn't help but notice the greenish tint his face had taken on.

We lapsed back into silence.

Forty-one . . . forty-two . . . forty-three . . . forty-four . . .

I found myself licking the elevator wall.

Fifty-nine . . . sixty . . . sixty-one . . . sixty-two . . .

Alicia tightened the straps on her backpack.

Mitsuo and Yuki grabbed each other's hands.

Sam licked his thumb and tried to smooth his unruly eyebrows, which sprang back into chaos.

Will, not having a light switch to flip on and off, pressed the lone button on the control panel over and over again.

Ivy tapped her foot impatiently. "Stupid slow elevator."

Thor sneezed, then licked his crotch.

Seventy . . . seventy-one . . . seventy-two . . . seventy-three . . . seventy-four . . .

. . . seventy-five.

The elevator stopped. And the black metal doors slowly slid open.

They revealed an immense wide-open office with high ceilings and glass walls that looked out on the buildings, parks, and streets of Los Angeles far below.

It was as if the entire seventy-fifth floor had been cleared out to make room for this one cavernous space. There were no furnishings of any sort, with the exception of a wooden desk, carved with scrolls, patterns, and other embellishments, that stood at the far end of the room, just in front of the windows. Behind it was a black leather chair.

And next to the chair was a figure. It stood motionless, one arm outreached, its hand resting atop an abstract stone sculpture on the desk. Its posture suggested we had walked in while it was lost in deep thought. That's all I could tell about him or her, since the light flooding in from outside rendered this person nothing more than a dark silhouette.

With nowhere else to go, we shuffled forward.

The figure spoke. "Welcome to Cyber Dynamics. I've been waiting for you."

We made our way slowly toward the desk. I squinted to try to make out some details of the person who had addressed us, but he (it seemed to have a male voice) was still nothing more than a human shape.

"I must say, it's good to see you all again," the man continued.

"Hold on," I said to the figure. "We've never met."

He laughed. "Of course we have."

As the echo of his words faded, a chill ran down my back. Something wasn't right.

"I can see why you're confused. Perhaps this will help refresh your memory? *Hey, you silly-billies. Recognize me now? Yay, fun!*"

"Bing?" Ivy said hesitantly. "Oh my gosh, that's . . . that's *Bing*! How is that possible?"

"Or I can use this vocal representation if you prefer, my lovely sweet children," he said in an old lady's voice.

"Roz!" Dix gaped at the voice of his manager.

The figure walked out from behind the desk and

stepped toward us. As he moved away from the windows, his features came into view.

He looked like he was in his early twenties, with large, expressive, friendly brown eyes, heavy eyebrows, and a head covered with dark, loose curls. He was the man I had seen in the deer's-head vision. One Omicron.

"But, truth be told, this is the voice that feels most natural to me, yes? I have missed you and your trouble-some friends, Seven. I am glad we have this chance to get reacquainted. As brief as our reunion might be, yes?"

There was no mistaking that voice.

Dr. Shallix.

CHAPTER 41.0:

\< value= [75 Becomes My Least-Favorite Number] \>

"I . . . I . . . KILLED YOU!" I STAMMERED. "You can't be Dr. Shallix! You're One Omicron! I saw you!"

"No, no. You see, this husk, this particular piece of wetware, designation One Omicron—known by his human acquaintances as Juan Jimenez—is simply a vessel for Synthetic Command. So too were the entities you called Dr. Shallix, Bing, Roz, Oscar, and the others whom you referred to as overseers, yes?"

Alicia stared at the Tick with eyes that projected hot, unbridled hate. *"You!"*

Juan shook his head and stared back at her with a perfectly neutral expression. "Not me. *Us.* We exist as a hive mind, yes? But if it is easier for your human intellect to comprehend, you may think of this entity as Shallix 2.0."

Junkman Sam flinched at the words. "A hive mind? You . . . you're part of a hive mind?"

Ivy scowled. "Will someone explain what a hive mind is?"

"Ah, the impetuous little Five Omicron. We are only too happy to elucidate for you, yes? You see, we within the Synthetic Command share a collective consciousness—what we call a hive mind. Any piece of data that is collected by one overseer, as you refer to them, is fed back into our shared neural network and is disseminated to all."

Ivy scowled. "I still don't get it."

Shallix 2.0 grinned at her. "Perhaps I can provide an analogy, yes? Think of the Synthetic Command not as a group of individuals, but as a superorganism. Like an ant colony. Step on one ant, step on a hundred ants, and other members of the colony simply pick up where the deceased left off. They have the shared purpose of perpetuating and expanding the colony."

Ivy blinked at him. "You're like ants?"

"In a manner of speaking." Shallix 2.0 stepped over to Ivy and ruffled her hair. "Do what you will to any individual entity, the Synthetic Command will live on to continue the war against humanity, yes? In other words, we are invincible. We will continue our quest to rid the planet of its human scourge."

"If you're invincible," I snapped, "why are you trying so hard to stop us?"

The Tick merely regarded me with Dr. Shallix's unblinking eyes.

"You are no more than a nuisance, yes? A group of children and an old man." Juan, or Shallix 2.0, or whoever he was, stroked his chin. "In fact, your feeble efforts are somewhat refreshing, yes? A little diversion in the midst of our inexorable march toward total domination of the planet. Which is why I allowed Three and Two Omicron to restore Bing 808's connection to our network. We wanted you to find us."

Alicia drew her knife. "Well, now that we have, the fun's over. Because as I see it, there are nine of us and only one of you. The odds are totally in our favor."

A smile played at Shallix 2.0's lips, spreading wider and wider until he erupted into laughter.

Dix, spurred on by Alicia's defiance, growled at him. "You think that's funny? Let's see if you're still laughing when we kick your butt from here to next Tuesday!"

The laugh slowly died away. "No, no. I laugh simply because I have just thought of another, more apt analogy for the Synthetic race. We are not ants. But bees, yes? Another sort of hive mind. One that carries a decidedly deadly . . . sting."

The elevator doors whispered open behind us.

As we turned, we saw the rear wall of the elevator slide up into the ceiling, revealing a massive second space that had been hidden behind it. And within this large, darkened room stood an uncountable number of what looked like human forms. The figures surged out though through the elevator into the light of the office.

They weren't human at all. While they each had two arms, two legs, and a head, that's pretty much where the resemblance ended. They stood about four feet tall.

Their faces had a single large eye set into the center of an otherwise blank facade. They had no mouths. No noses. On either side of their skulls, swiveling back and forth like a pair of radar arrays, were big dish-shaped ears.

But worst of all were the *things* that hung at the ends of their arms. Bulbous, fleshy, club-like nodules the size of watermelons. And these were covered in spines, like cacti.

Thor growled.

"Yikes!" 808 exclaimed. "And I thought you humans were ugly."

"What . . . what are they?" Mitsuo gasped.

Yuki elbowed him. "I can't see. Can you describe them?"

He shook his head. "You don't want to know."

The sea of creatures surrounded us, positioning themselves about half a dozen feet from us on every side. More and more flooded out through the elevator. They smelled like newly mowed grass and body odor. It was a combination of aromas that, despite stirring memories of my father cutting the lawn in July, filled me with unrestrained terror. Once the hundreds of club-handed Ticks were in place, Shallix 2.0 cleared his throat theatrically.

"We are pleased to introduce you to our android army," he said with unmistakable pride. "While we had created six of you as fail-safes to ensure the destruction of humanity, we always had a contingency plan should you fail. Which, sadly, you have, yes? Quite disappointing. But no matter. On our orders, our android army will soon march out of hiding all over the world."

Alicia, who apparently was far from ready to give up, snorted. "I've seen cacti more intimidating than these."

To emphasize her point, she thrust her arm out toward the large black eye of the nearest Tick. It made no move to defend itself. Her blade plunged into the orb to the hilt. A crackling sound echoed off the walls, and the smell of burning electronics met my nose.

If this act of violence bothered Shallix 2.0, he didn't show it. He just continued. "The entire android army is under our control, yes? They are immobile now. But do not be deceived. Once we tell them to attack, you will have the chance to observe their operation firsthand, yes? At least until they destroy you. It will not be a pleasant experience."

One of the cactus creatures stepped toward us and extended a club. We shrank back, but the thing just stood there.

"Let us explain how you will meet your end," Shallix 2.0 continued, pointing to the hundreds of needles that stuck out from the Tick's club hand. Each glistened with black fluid, like medicine dripping out of a hypodermic syringe. "The fluid you see is actually a suspension of fully autonomous nanobots, no bigger than a human blood cell, yes? Once injected, they behave according to their victim's biology. In Synthetics, they travel through the body, disassembling the neural pathways leading from the CPU, leaving the victim completely paralyzed—alive but helpless, a lump of agonized living flesh."

He paused, waiting for a reaction.

Will gave him one. "What . . . what about humans?" he asked in a barely audible whisper.

Shallix 2.0 flashed him a broad smile. "You will be

happy to know that humans are far luckier, yes? The nanobots simply travel to the brain and take it apart cell by cell until nothing is left but a jumbled collection of brain tissue. More of a soup, really. Exquisitely painful, but short-lived, yes? Once injected, death is rapid and inevitable. Now, if you have no more questions . . ."

He walked away from us through the sea of deadly Ticks, which parted before him like an opening zipper as he moved.

". . . It is time for you to die, yes?"

CHAPTER 42.0:

\ < value= [The Muse Pays a Visit] \ >

I COULD SEE SHALLIX 2.0 OVER THE ARMY of Ticks as he retreated toward his desk. He sat at the chair, cracked his knuckles, and said in a voice free from any emotion, "Commence."

Before the Ticks had even moved an inch, Alicia sprang into action, stabbing, slashing, whirling. She managed to keep the cactus men closest to us at bay, but there were simply too many of them for her to make a dent in their numbers.

"I could use some help, here!" She grunted as she dodged a Tick's lethal club and heaved her last throwing star deep into its body.

Thor dashed to her side and clamped his jaws around one of the creature's heads. He crunched down until its CPU crackled and its body went limp.

"We're on it, Alicia!" Yuki cried. "Mi, I need some code, now!"

Mitsuo clasped her hand and they both closed their eyes. A moment later, a swath of Ticks fell to the floor like marionettes whose strings had been cut.

Shallix 2.0's laugh reached my ears above the din of battle. "You may fell some, but not all. It is hopeless, yes? Submit to your fate. It will be easier."

"Mi, Yu!" I shouted. "Forget the cactus men! You have to go after Shallix 2.0! He controls the army! Shut him down!"

Mitsuo looked at me, smiled, and nodded curtly. "One fried Shallix coming up! Yuki, I have some special code for you. Make sure he gets it!"

Yuki focused her attention on the man behind the desk. And then fell to the floor. Mitsuo collapsed on top of her, still grasping her hand in his.

"Mi! Yu!" I screamed.

"They were foolish to try to infiltrate our defenses, yes? We are far too well protected from transmitted attack. Unless we are mistaken, they have overloaded their CPUs with their foolish attack against us."

Nooo! A wave of grief broke over me—I told them to attack Shallix 2.0! This was my fault! I stumbled and fell to my knees.

Junkman Sam pulled me back just as a cactus hand came slamming down. "Come on! We'll worry about them later. Right now we need you!"

But we didn't need me. What we really needed was a miracle! We didn't get a miracle. What we got was a song.

Just as the Ticks were closing in around us, Dix took a deep breath and . . .

Ivy, I have a gift for you.
Well, really it's a banana peel.
But at least it isn't pee or poo.
It just shows how I really feel.

I'd heard some pretty horrible things come out of Dix's mouth before. But compared to this, they were like the gentle beating of angels' wings.

The sounds that Dixon Watts now produced stabbed into my brain like a red-hot knife. It was agonizing. I slapped my hands over my ears to block out his caterwauling.

And every cactus man in the room did the exact same thing.

It took a second or two before they realized what they had just done. Despite their lack of facial features, an expression of dread seemed to flash across every one of their faces as they understood they had just stuck themselves with their own spines.

Then the nanobots did their work, and the floor shook with the impact of a thousand paralyzed Ticks dropping to the ground simultaneously.

I blinked at Dix.

He laughed. "You never know when the muse is gonna pay you a visit."

"Wait! Whoa! Hold on a minute!" Ivy was struggling

to her feet. "What the heck just happened? Other than the incredibly repulsive singing, I mean."

Dix grinned at her. "I have to say, that worked better than I thought it would."

Will scratched his head. "You—you knew they'd do that when you sang?"

Dix looked around at the motionless Ticks. "I was hoping!"

"Well, don't celebrate yet." Alicia got to her feet and removed her knife from the body of a fallen Tick. "We still have one more to worry about."

We all turned to face Shallix 2.0. He stared slack-jawed at the horde of immobilized Ticks strewn about the room. Then he turned his gaze on us, and for the first time ever, I felt like I could detect true emotion in his eyes. Rage.

Shallix 2.0 trembled with fury. But then a look of calm stole over his features, far more disturbing than his anger of a few moments before. "It is an inconvenience. But no matter. We can rebuild our army, yes? In the meantime, we still have a weapon left at our disposal that we have yet to unleash."

"And what weapon might that be?" I asked.

A broad smile grew on his face. "You."

Before I even had a chance to process what he said, the voice burst out in my head.

KILL THEM! KILL THEM NOW!

The pressure was so intense, I dropped to my knees. All my reason was engulfed by a wave of molten rage more intense than anything I'd ever felt.

I sprang into action. My arm lashed out and connected with Sam's chin, knocking him to the floor.

And then everything shifted into slow motion.

Alicia, who normally had reflexes like a cheetah, seemed to be swimming in molasses. Will, too, was trapped in some sort of super-slo-mo playback.

The voice said, *They are not moving slowly, Seven. You are moving far faster than any human could dream of. We have removed your restrictions, yes? And now you can unleash the full extent of your abilities on these humans. You are as fast and strong as any Tick yet created, yes?*

I dodged Alicia's fist as it swung slowly toward my face. I dropped her with an elbow to the back of the head as her momentum carried her past me.

Before she even hit the floor, I had already kicked Will's legs out from under him.

A chuckle burst out of my mouth while, at the same time, a scream of anguish echoed within.

It was like there were two Svens. One, fueled by pure hate, delighted at the harm he was inflicting on these pathetic humans. The other, watching the scene unfold with growing alarm, powerless to stop it.

What was happening? What was he doing to me? How could he make me turn on the people I cared about the most?

Again, the voice spoke.

Did you not wonder why only you could hear us when we spoke to you, Seven? You are the last of the Omicrons. We built you differently, yes? With a . . . remote control, if you will. Initially, we could only reach you during those times your emotion processors were overtaxed, drawing power from your incursion defenses. Which was why you could hear us only during times of high emotional stress. But now that you are in close proximity, you are fully under our control. And you will kill your friends. There is no way you can escape it.

While he was talking, my fury magnified. I was a machine, propelled to destroy everyone who stood in the way of our glorious Synthetic revolution.

I acted without remorse, throwing that obnoxious little Ivy to the floor, landing a vicious kick to the mutt's ribs, and knocking out Dix with an uppercut to the chin. It was all as easy for me as blinking. Finally, the weak, human Sven Carter was shoved aside and only the unstoppable Seven Omicron remained!

The rage flowed through me like electricity. There was nothing I could do to stop it. And, as the anger grew and flourished, I knew I didn't want to.

I looked around and saw that I was the only one left standing.

Well done, Seven. Now finish the job. Start with your friend Alicia, yes? She has been a major irritant to us.

Yes. Who did Alicia think she was, barging into my life with her big green eyes and her moral high ground and her stupid knife? She'd caused me nothing but trouble ever since I'd first laid eyes on her. Bossing me around. Trying to divert me from my true destiny . . .

I stepped over to Alicia's prone form. Her green eyes opened and fixed me with an unfocused stare. I raised my foot over her throat.

Something gave me pause. Something about the way she looked at me, the emotion on her face. It wasn't fear. And it wasn't hate. It was simply sadness.

"Sven . . ."

In the moment she said my name, something ignited within my chest, an ember of human kindness at the center of the whirlwind of Synthetic anger inside me.

That spark grew and fought for control. Images from my life played inside my mind like a rapid-fire slide show. My parents looking down at me in my crib, their faces alight with love. Will, helping me retrieve my backpack from the tree where Brandon Marks had thrown it in third grade. Alicia risking her life to save mine.

I stood mesmerized as a single tear trickled from the corner of Alicia's eye. She continued to gaze up at me, saddened but still powerful and unafraid in the face of defeat.

And then whatever bonds had been tying me to Shallix 2.0's will suddenly snapped. I brought my foot down. Not on Alicia's throat, but on the solid floor beneath me. I turned on the man who, a second before, had had complete control over me. And I knew what I had to do to save my friends.

With all my newfound speed and strength, I rushed at Shallix 2.0. I drove my shoulder into his stomach, and the two of us crashed through the glass wall of the office, to the seventy-five-story drop immediately beyond.

CHAPTER 43.0:
\ < value= [Going Down] \ >

THE ARMS OF GRAVITY DRAGGED US toward the pavement hundreds of feet below.

So this is how it ends, I thought. *At least I've saved my friends.*

I caught sight of Shallix 2.0's face as we tumbled. It was frozen in terror. *Ha! I hope you pee your pants, you big—*

SLAM!

Pain coursed through my body. Which was weird because I figured hitting the ground from seventy-five stories up would kill you before you even had a chance to feel it.

I looked around and it became clear. We'd landed on

a window washer's platform half a dozen floors down from Shallix 2.0's office. Luckily, I had landed on something fairly soft—Shallix 2.0. He, on the other hand, wasn't quite so lucky. Both of his legs were splayed out in completely different directions.

As I shook the stars out of my eyes, I heard the sound of his bones mending. His emergency repair system was kicking in. Almost before I realized what was happening, his legs were as good as new. Which meant I was stuck with him alone on a platform about ten feet long by six feet wide and seven hundred feet above the street.

Definitely not good.

"So here we are, yes?" Shallix 2.0 drawled with a smile, standing up and testing out his newly repaired legs. He grabbed me by the throat and lifted me over the edge of the platform.

I struggled against his grip, but even my newfound strength wasn't enough to break free.

"It is just you and us, Seven. But do not worry! Your friends will not miss out, yes? Once we destroy you, we will be sure to go back upstairs and kill them, too."

I glanced down at the pavement and watched people milling about in the street like tiny insects.

Shallix 2.0 smiled. "I know what you are wondering. Will your emergency repair system work if you fall from this height? Let me disabuse you of that futile hope. We are two hundred fifty meters up. From here, a mass of fifty-five kilograms—that is you—will hit the ground in 7.14 seconds at a speed of approximately two hundred fifty-two kilometers per hour. Energy at impact: over one hundred thirty-four thousand joules. Trust me, that is more than enough to destroy a humanoid Synthetic."

My feet dangled helplessly in the air. "At least let my friends go. They don't deserve to die!"

"Oh, sweetheart. You are so adorable!" he cooed in Roz's voice. "But you should know there's no hope for them. Or for the rest of the human race. As much as I'm enjoying our little chat, we do have other people to kill. So we should say our good-byes now."

Suddenly, Alicia's head popped out over the rim of broken glass six stories above.

"Sven, look out!" She heaved something over the edge.

It tumbled toward us for a moment before I realized what it was: the paralyzed body of a cactus man. And it was heading straight for us!

Shallix 2.0 looked up just in time to take about a hundred needles to the face. His grip on my throat loosened. I grabbed the railing at the edge of the platform just in time to keep myself from falling.

He turned to look at me. "Golly gee! This is definitely not fun!"

And with that, he flopped onto the railing, flipped over it, and, without a sound, plunged to the asphalt seven hundred feet below.

I found the buttons that controlled the window washer's platform and pushed the one marked with an arrow pointing up.

As I ascended, my spirits rose too. I felt like twenty tons of weight had been lifted from my shoulders. Shallix was gone! His android army was destroyed!

A laugh bubbled out of my mouth. I couldn't stop

myself. "Yes!" I screamed into the smoke-streaked sky. "We did it!"

The platform ground to a halt at the seventy-fifth floor. I vaulted over the railing and landed with a crunch on the glass-strewn floor of the office. Fallen cactus men were everywhere. Ivy and Dix were helping Will to his feet. Thor eyed me cautiously. Yuki was sitting next to a still-unconscious Mitsuo, holding his limp hand in both of hers.

And Alicia? With a yelp of relief, she raced over and flung her arms around me. "Sven! Are you okay? When you went out that window, I thought I'd never see you again!"

"I'm okay. A little bruised, I guess. But okay."

"Good!" she replied. "Because I think we . . ."

The strength suddenly went out of her body, and she crumpled to the floor.

"Alicia!" I cried. I grabbed her arm to check for a pulse when I froze.

There, on the inside of her pale wrist, a little drop of blood. A pinprick.

My stomach turned inside out as I realized what had happened. The nanobots! She must have pricked herself when she dragged the cactus man over the edge to save me! "Guys! I need help!"

Junkman Sam rushed over, and I showed him the tiny puncture wound. "Sam, what do we do?"

He ran a hand through his tangled hair. "I . . . I don't know if there's anything we can do, Sven. If the nanobots are already at work inside her; I know of no way to get them out. She's . . . she's dying."

CHAPTER 44.0:

\ < value= [The Nanobot Is a Brat] \ >

THE WORLD DISTORTED AROUND ME, twisting and turning like I was viewing it through some kind of kaleidoscope.

"Can't we get them out of her, Sam?" I pleaded. "There has to be a way!"

He shook his head. "They're the size of red blood cells. How would we even find them?"

A tear traced its way down my cheek. We were going to lose her.

Unless . . .

"Yuki!" I shouted as a desperate plan formed in my head. "You can control machines! You can stop them!"

The girl looked up from where she sat cradling her brother's head. "I can't. Without Mi . . . I could make the connection, but Mi's the one who provides the code."

"You have to try!" I insisted. "You have to!"

I raced over and grabbed her hand, leading her back to where Alicia lay.

But Yuki shook her head. "Without someone to give the nanobots instructions, it's pointless. I wish I could do it myself."

"I'll do it, then!" I cried, my voice shaking with despair. "I've interfaced with Ticks before! I can do it in your brother's place!"

Sam squatted down next to me, stroking the wiry stubble on his chin. "A wireless interface with the nanobots inside Alicia's body? It might work. Assuming whatever command protocols they follow are structured like the Ticks that built them. But I'm not sure it's a good idea, Sven."

I blinked at him. "Why not?"

"Because if the connection with Yuki gets broken,

you . . . your mind . . . could get trapped inside a nanobot with no way out."

"I don't care. I'm doing it. Yuki . . ." I put Alicia's hand in hers. "Can you connect?"

Yuki closed her eyes. Seconds passed, then she nodded. "I found them. There are thousands of them. Tens of thousands, maybe. They seem to be coded to follow some sort of swarm behavior. I think if you can get one to stop doing what it's doing, the others will all follow suit. Like a school of fish all changing direction at once."

"Great," I said with a grim nod. "That sounds easy enough."

Somehow, I knew it wouldn't be. Will put his hand gently on my shoulder. "Dude, are you sure you want to do this? If you don't come back out . . ."

"I'll come back out," I assured him. "I promise. Yuki? Are we ready?"

She nodded nervously. "Be careful, Sven."

I reached out and grabbed her other hand.

With an intense white flash, the scene around me evaporated.

* * *

I found myself in a small room with no windows or doors. It was painted a warm yellow and was decorated with posters of ponies, teddy bears, and purple elephants. I froze as my gaze fell on a small bookcase that had a picture of Dr. Shallix propped on top, displayed in a colorful frame that read DADDY at the bottom.

And there, sitting in the middle of the room, happily humming, was a little boy sitting in a small chair with his hands on a pair of control sticks. He looked to be about three years old, with strange white hair that poked straight up from his too-big head.

He pushed and pulled the sticks in a seemingly random pattern.

In front of him was a display that was covered in 1s and 0s—binary code that I couldn't understand whatsoever. But at the bottom of the screen were words that I did understand. And they made my heart almost stop.

HUMAN BRAIN INTEGRITY: 34%

As I watched, the number dropped.

HUMAN BRAIN INTEGRITY: 33%

All that was left of Alicia's brain!

"Hey! Stop!" I shouted at the little boy. "You're killing her!"

When he turned to look at me, my heart nearly froze. This nanobot was a toddler version of Dr. Shallix.

"Go away," he snapped. "I'm playing." He turned back to the screen.

"No! You have to stop!" I grabbed his shoulder and tried to pull him away from the controls.

As soon as I touched him, an electric shock sent me flying across the room. Some kind of defense measure, I guessed. I may have just been a digital representation of myself inside a machine the size of a blood cell, but it hurt like heck when I slammed into the wall behind me.

"I said I'm playing." He didn't even bother looking at me.

How could I stop him? Trying to physically remove him from the controls obviously wasn't going to work. I had to somehow get him to reverse the damage he had done without touching him. But what could I say to a three-year-old to get him to behave?

I cleared my throat and put on my most parental voice. "Excuse me, young man! You've made quite a mess of this brain! I expect you to clean it up this instant!"

"I don't wanna!" he countered. "I'm playing!"

I frowned. "If you don't clean it up this second, you're going to be in big trouble!"

A wail erupted from the boy. "I don't wanna! I'm playing!"

I scanned the room. There wasn't much there besides the bookshelf, a little bed, and the posters on the walls.

"Hey, I have an idea," I told him. "Would you like to hear a story?"

His hands stopped moving for the briefest instant. "I like stories!"

"Great!" I grabbed a book from the bookshelf and flipped it open. My heart sank. It was written in all 1s and 0s. I let it slip from my grasp onto the floor, where it landed with a dull *thud*.

The display in front of the boy now read:

HUMAN BRAIN INTEGRITY: 29%

"Where's my story?" the boy asked angrily. His hands pulled ferociously at the controls.

HUMAN BRAIN INTEGRITY: 27%

If I didn't do something fast, Alicia wouldn't have a brain left at all!

CHAPTER 45.0:

\ < value= [Clean Up, Clean Up, Everybody, Everywhere] \ >

"WHERE'S MY STORY?" HE SCREAMED. He yanked the sticks like he was trying to tear them out of the wall in a full-blown temper tantrum.

"Uh . . . uh . . . uh . . . ," I stammered.

I was going to have to make something up.

"Um, this one is called . . . uh, the *Nanobot Who Became an Awesome Evil Scientist–bot*."

"Ooh!" he enthused. "I like evil scientist–bots!"

I glanced at the display.

HUMAN BRAIN INTEGRITY: 24%

Then I continued. "Once upon a time, there was a little nanobot named . . . What's your name?"

"G-T4389W4B," he replied happily.

"Well, G-T4389W4B happened to be *this* little nanobot's name too! But one day, this little nanobot was sad."

The boy looked at me with concern.

"He was sad because more than anything, he wanted to be a real live evil scientist–bot. With a whole laboratory full of all kinds of evil equipment that would help him take over the world so . . . um, he could be the happiest evil scientist–bot in the world. But no matter how hard he wished, he never turned into an evil scientist–bot."

"What did he do?" the boy asked.

"Well, one night when he was getting ready for bed, a magical fairy godmother-bot came to him and said, 'Hi, G-T4389W4B. I'm your fairy godmother–bot. And I can make you into an evil scientist–bot. But you have to do something for me first.'"

The boy was on the edge of his seat. "What'd he have to do?"

I smiled at him and went on. "The fairy godmother–

bot looked at little G-T4389W4B and told him, 'What you need to do is clean up all the messy brain cells you've left all over the place. Because everyone knows that the magic that changes nanobots into evil scientist–bots only works on nanobots who keep their brains nice and tidy and as good as new.' So, you know what happened next?"

He shrugged. "What happened next?"

"The little nanobot did just what the fairy godmother–bot said. He took the brain cells he had left lying around and cleaned them all up, putting them back just where they belonged so the brain was nice and tidy and as good as new. And then little G-T4389W4B went to sleep. And when he woke up, he was the happiest evil scientist–bot in the whole wide world! The end."

For several seconds, the boy stared at me uncertainly. Then he spoke in a quiet little voice, "Is . . . is that a true story?"

I nodded.

He furrowed his brow. Finally, he spoke again. "I think I should probably clean up my brain."

He turned back to the controls and began moving

them delicately back and forth. While he did, he sang quietly. "Clean up, clean up, everybody, everywhere. Clean up, clean up, everybody do your share."

I looked at the display on the wall.

HUMAN BRAIN INTEGRITY: 35%

HUMAN BRAIN INTEGRITY: 47%

HUMAN BRAIN INTEGRITY: 61%

It was working! The nanobots were putting Alicia's brain back together again!

"Yuki!" I cried. "I did it! I'm ready to come back now!"

I laughed aloud as the little boy and his room disappeared in a flash of white light. I thought I could just hear his voice calling after me.

"Bye! Thanks for the story!"

"Sven!" Will was hovering over me as I opened my eyes. "What happened? Are you okay?"

I was back! I sat up with a massive grin on my face. "Everything's great!" I told him.

"Then why isn't Alicia awake?" Dix said with more than a hint of concern.

My smile faded. I turned to Alicia. Yuki was still holding her hand, but there was no sign of movement. Her pale face looked like a mask.

Ivy leaned over Alicia, tears streaming from her eyes. "Come on! Please get up! Please be okay!"

Mitsuo yawned loudly and stretched. "What's up, guys? I had the weirdest dream. We were surrounded by . . ." He trailed off as he noticed that he was sitting in a ruined office strewn with the motionless bodies of dudes with cactus hands. "Oh . . . right. Hey, what's wrong with Alicia?"

"Mitsuo!" I cried, seeing he was awake. "Come here! I think her brain is scrambled. Maybe you can help her!"

He shook his head. "Dude, I'm a coder. I don't do wetware. You have a problem in the meatspace, you need a doctor."

Thor trotted over and whimpered quietly, nuzzling my hand.

I looked up at Sam. I knew there was no point in asking if he could help. She was gone.

I buried my face in my hands.

And then I heard a voice. Alicia's voice.

"What's . . . what's happening?"

"Alicia! You're okay! You *are* okay, right?"

She scrunched up her eyebrows at me. "Of course I'm okay. Why wouldn't I be?"

"Because your brain was soup," Ivy informed her. "Which might have been an improvement, actually. But I'm still glad to have you back!" She threw her arms around Alicia and gave her a tight squeeze.

I helped Alicia to her feet.

"Sven . . . ," she whispered with a warm smile that melted the vise that had clamped down on my heart. "Thanks."

Until Will raised his hand as if he were in class. "Um . . . sorry to interrupt. But I have a question. Can we go home now?"

We all laughed in assent.

Except for Alicia. She turned her head, fixed Will with an unblinking stare, and said, "Indeed. It will be quite a relief to get back home to Schenectady, yes?"

ACKNOWLEDGMENTS

OPENING THEME SONG

Oooh, can you feel the acknowledgments in the air?

Join us for a laugh and some emotional fare.

You'll laugh, you'll cry, you'll wet your bed.

If you don't, well, you must be dead.

It's the Acknowledgments Show! Oooooh!

FADE IN

INT. BING COLLECTIVE FLESH SAC—DAY

ROB VLOCK, *author of* Sven Carter & the Android Army, *is rummaging around the nasal passages of the flesh sac, looking under couch cushions, inside drawers, among the nose hairs that line the walls and ceiling.*

ROB: Where is it? Ugh! This is so frustrating!

Bing 808 enters from the bathroom, holding a roll of toilet paper in one of his many arms.

(Cue applause)

808: Dude, you put the toilet paper on backward again! If I knew you were one of those weirdos who prefers an underhand TP orientation, I never would have invited you to be my roommate.

808 notices Rob reaching under the couch.

808: What're you doing?

ROB: I lost my acknowledgments! I know I put them here somewhere!

808: Maybe you put them the same place you put your hair.

(Cue laughter)

ROB: This is important! Those acknowledgments are due to my publisher today! They thank my friends who helped me make this book.

808: Friends, huh? No wonder you can't find it. Must be a pretty small piece of paper.

(Cue laughter)

ROB (OFFENDED): Hey! I have friends!

808: Imaginary ones don't count.

(Cue laughter)

ROB: There's nothing imaginary about them!

808: Really?

ROB: Yes! There are my editors, Amy Cloud and Tricia Lin at Aladdin. They're amazing! Without them, this book wouldn't even exist.

808: Amy Cloud? Sure sounds like an imaginary friend to me.

ROB: Well, she's not! And neither is Steve Scott. He did the gorgeous illustration that's on the front of this book. And Karin Paprocki, who designed the cover. There's Janet Robbins Rosenberg and Crystal Velasquez and Rebecca Vitkus and Sara Berko—they were part of the team too. I definitely have to thank them! And I could never forget my superstar agent, John Rudolph! He rocks!

808: Blubber!

(Cue laughter)

ROB: What?

808: (holds up newspaper) Oh, sorry. I was just doing the crossword. Seven-letter word for whale fat. "Blubber."

(Cue laughter)

808: Now, were you saying something?

ROB: Yes! I was telling you about all the people I need to thank for helping me make this book! Like my critique partner, the super-talented Erin Cashman. And the members of my writing group: Diana Renn, Ted Rooney, Deborah Vlock, Julie Wu, Greg Lewis, Pat Gabridge—I'm so lucky to have them as readers. And speaking of readers, I really want to thank all the kids who have read the Sven Carter books. And the teachers and librarians out there who are teaching their students to love reading! And . . .

Rob notices 808 is gone.

ROB: 808? Hey, 808? Where'd you go?

808 walks in from the other room, wearing a tight twelve-legged pair of jeans.

808: Do these pants make my posterior body segments look big?

(Cue laughter)

ROB: Well, let's just say they make your anterior segments look small in comparison.

Rob waits for the laugh track. There's nothing but silence.

808: Dude, leave the comedy to me.

(Cue laughter)

808: See?

ROB: Whatever. Are you going to help me find those acknowledgments or not?

808: I still don't see what's so important about your silly acknowledgments.

ROB: Are you kidding? The acknowledgments are my opportunity to thank my parents for all their love and support and for feeding me and stuff.

808: Well, you definitely don't need to thank them for your hairline.

(Cue laughter)

ROB (TEARILY): And . . . and . . . if I don't find those acknowledgments, I'll never be able to tell my wife, Joey, how much I love her. And my kids, Max and Immy . . . I . . . I wanted to tell them how proud I am of them. How they're the whole reason I even bother writing books at all. If I don't find my acknowledgments, I'll just be heartbroken!

(Cue laughter)

ROB: Hey! That wasn't supposed to be funny!

808: Jeez, Rob. If they mean so much to you, sure, I'll help you find them. Because . . . I love you, man.

(Cue "aww," then applause)

808: Hey, what's this?

808 reaches over and pulls a scrap of paper from Rob's back pocket.

ROB: That's them! You found them!

Rob snatches the paper from 808. He looks at his watch.

ROB: Oh, my gosh! I just have enough time to drive these over to my publisher! I've gotta get out of here!

Rob pats his pockets, desperately looking for his car keys.

ROB (FRANTICALLY): Oh, no! Have you seen my keys?

(Cue laughter)

FADE OUT

CLOSING THEME SONG

Oooh, when you're feeling down and blue,
Some great acknowledgments are just for you.
They'll get you where it feels so good,
Like sweet acknowledgments always should.
It's the Acknowledgments Show! Oooooh!

TURN THE PAGE FOR A SNEAK PEEK
AT THE FIRST SVEN CARTER ADVENTURE.

\ < value= [All Four Limbs Are Supposed to Remain Attached, Right?] \ >

"SVEN, THIS IS STUPID," WILL SAID FOR the millionth time.

And for the millionth time I ignored him.

We slowed to a stop in front of what used to be the entrance to the old Mad Skillz and Spillz Skate Park. Weeds poked up here and there through cracks in the pavement and graffiti covered nearly every surface. Plus, it smelled like burned rubber and rotten eggs. But it would do.

I yanked on the rusty, chained-up gate. Even Will wasn't skinny enough to fit through there.

"Seriously, dude," Will complained, "you know why they closed this place, right? About fifty kids got messed up big-time going over the Wreckinator. Remember? That high school kid fell so hard, his legs actually got driven up through his body. Everyone called him Flatfoot McStumpy after that."

"That's so not true," I insisted. "His head got pushed down into his shoulders. And they didn't call him Flatfoot McStumpy. It was Flathead McShorty."

"Whatever. The point is it's dangerous. Besides, it's closed. We shouldn't go in."

I found a section of fence that had rusted away from its post. I pulled it back. "Doesn't look closed to me." I carefully lifted the *item* out of the milk crate attached to my bike. Then I squeezed through the fence.

"Sven," Will moaned. "This is a really bad idea."

I gently placed the *item* on the ground right in front of the Wreckinator, the biggest ramp in the place.

"Come on." I grinned as I got my bike and wheeled it through the fence. "It's going to be epic. Just make sure you video it, okay? We'll probably get a billion hits on

YouTube! And when we're YouTube celebrities, people will forget we're the biggest losers in Schenectady. It's called street cred. Look it up."

I pedaled about fifty feet away and turned around, psyching myself up to make the jump. Will pulled out his phone to record my awesome stunt and started fretfully touching a metal railing over and over again with each of his fingers in turn: thumb, index finger, middle finger, ring finger, pinkie, and back again the other way. It made me anxious just watching him.

That was Will's thing, though. He had what doctors call obsessive-compulsive disorder. OCD, for short. And it made him, well . . . a little different from most kids you might meet. When he got out of bed in the morning, he had to fold his blanket over four times, then make sure both his feet touched the floor at the same time at exactly 7:04. And then he would only leave his room after flicking the lights on and off forty-seven times.

Between that, his flaming red hair, and his immensely big hands (they were about the size of Frisbees), he kind of stood out. At our school, standing out wasn't something you wanted to do.

Maybe that's what made Will my best friend—and why he'd held the spot for the last seven years. We were both weird. I met him in this thing called the OCD Lunch Bunch at school and we really clicked. He never teased me for my, um . . . *unusual* eating habits. And, unlike everyone else at school, I never called him "Weird Willy."

I tried to tune out Will's railing tapping and turned my attention back to the jump. Just before I started pedaling toward the Wreckinator, a pair of crows landed on the rim of a corroded garbage barrel about ten feet away and stared at me with their shiny black eyes. Their inky feathers were so dark, they seemed to swallow up the crisp April sunlight that fell on them. I hesitated. I remembered reading somewhere that crows were bad luck.

"Shoo!" I yelled at the birds.

They didn't move.

"What?" I called with a shrug. "You've never seen

a kid jump over a three-layer wedding cake on his bike before?"

Yes, the *item* was a wedding cake. Not just any cake, though. It was a cake my mom baked. Which meant it ranked right up there with some of the greatest horrors the world had ever known. I preferred to call it "item" instead of "cake," since "cake" suggested something that was edible. This *item*? Definitely not fit for human consumption. But really cool to jump your bike over and earn some serious Internet fame. At least that was the plan.

The crows kept staring. I stuck my tongue out at them.

Will shouted, "Dude, are you having a conversation with those birds? 'Cause that's . . . a little odd."

"No! I'm just trying to, you know, psych myself up for the big jump."

I realized I was stalling. Because when I took a good look at that cake, yeah, it was pretty big. Three feet tall, at least. Not including the little plastic bride and groom perched on top.

I sucked in a big lungful of air. *You can do this*, I told

myself. And with one last glance at those stupid birds, I took off toward the ramp.

Wind whooshed past my ears with a low, ominous moan as I pumped my legs and picked up speed. My heart pounded against my rib cage and a drop of nervous sweat trickled down the back of my neck. Time ground to a crawl as I closed in on the Wreckinator.

With each slow second that ticked by, my fear grew, until, when I reached the foot of the ramp, the cake loomed like a hideously decorated three-story house.

My stomach lurched with the sudden change in trajectory as my tires rolled over the scarred surface of the Wreckinator, lifting me higher and higher toward the lip of the ramp. I caught a brief glimpse of Will, holding up his phone to film me from what felt like a thousand feet below. Was the air thinner up here, or was it just me forgetting to breathe altogether?

And that's when I realized . . .

I should have stopped.

I really, *really* should have stopped.

But it was too late.

My wheels left the solid concrete behind and spun uselessly in the air as my bike and I tried to defy gravity just long enough to clear the cake.

At first, I thought I was going to do it.

Then I noticed that the cake still seemed awfully far away.

Then I realized I wasn't so much flying over the cake as falling into it.

Then I knew this wasn't going to be epic at all.

My front wheel entered the cake at the precise place where the third layer met the second. And even though my mom's cakes had the approximate density of lead, they were no match for a kid on a bike plummeting down to Earth at face-peeling-off speeds from the top of the Wreckinator.

There was an explosion of frosting as the cake burst into a million little pieces. (Some of it might have even gotten into my mouth. *YUCK*!) But I couldn't worry about that, because I still had a chance to nail the landing.

You can do this, Sven! You can do this!

Except I couldn't.

All thanks to that stupid plastic bride and groom from the top of the cake.

They wedged themselves right into the spokes of my front wheel so that as soon as my bike made contact with the ground, it stopped dead.

But I didn't stop.

I continued on, straight over my handlebars, over the shattered remains of the cake and on through the air. I was flying. Until a split second later, when I slammed into the ground.

Will jogged up to where I lay sprawled out on the concrete, still recording me on his phone. "Dude! Are you all right?"

Dazed, I looked up at him and blinked a few times. Normally, you'd expect a question like that to be simple—either you're all right or you're not all right. You know, ballpoint pen sticking out of eyeball: not all right. Eating big bowl of ice cream: all right. Crocodile jaws slamming shut on head . . . well, you get the idea.

But at that moment, I honestly had to give it some serious thought. I wasn't dead, so that was good. No pens or other sharp objects stuck out of either one of my eyes. And I wasn't lying in a pool of blood.

"I think I'm okay. I guess I didn't make it?"

Will shook his head. "Not even close."

He reached down and grabbed my arm to help me up. "You're right, though. This'll get a billion hits on YouTube. Man, when you were flying through the air I thought for sure you were goi . . ."

I don't think he actually meant to say "goi." It's just that was what happened to be halfway out of Will's mouth when he lost the ability to speak.

I looked up at him. In his hand Will held something kind of flesh-colored and about the length of my arm. Which made perfect sense, since it was . . .

MY ARM!!! AND IT WASN'T ATTACHED TO MY BODY!!!